And the Sons of Ham

Marcella Denise Spencer

And the Sons of Ham

ISBN 978-0-9843624-0-0

The Great
Sea

Canaan

Phut

Mizraim

Arabia

Red
Sea

Napata

Cush

Sennar

Punt

Table of Contents

"In the year that Tartan came unto Ashdod, (when Sargon the king of Assyria sent him,) and fought against Ashdod, and took it; At the same time spake the LORD by Isaiah the son of Amoz, saying, Go and loose the sackcloth from off thy loins, and put off thy shoe from thy foot. And he did so, walking naked and barefoot. And the LORD said, Like as my servant Isaiah hath walked naked and barefoot three years for a sign and wonder upon Egypt and upon Ethiopia; So shall the king of Assyria lead away the Egyptians prisoners, and the Ethiopians captives, young and old, naked and barefoot, even with their buttocks uncovered, to the shame of Egypt. – Isaiah 20: 1-5

Prologue

I know. Many of you will not believe this story. And no matter how much I say it's true, you still won't believe me. I can see some of you now. Heads cocked, looking at me cross-eyed. Some of you are shaking your heads, thinking, "Lord Jesus, that brother sure needs your help."

I'm probably the only brother that can trace his ancestry back to the beginning. Seriously. And I didn't do it by research. I didn't spend hours in a library squinting at census records.

I prayed.

No joke. I prayed my way back to the cradle of civilization. The Nile Valley. And yes, this is the book about it. I know some of you are already asking, "Why? What started this quest?" Well, an innocent question from one of my students led me to my great-great-grandmother Sadie, which led me to her ancestors ...

Father Ham
3900 BC

Mule-drawn caravans traveling in double strand slowed to a halt. Young boys let out fierce yelps and frog-leaped off the wagons. They raced each other toward the Nile River. The older boys helped the men who were leading the longhorn cattle toward a grassy area.

Dusk's rosy glow suggested an evening meal. Babies' wails pierced the air. A wild animal shrieked. The young girls congregated around their mothers. The women grabbed small hands and split into groups. Some unrolled animal skins to pitch tents. Others took flax baskets and went in search of fruit-bearing trees and herbs.

Ham stood at the riverbank staring at the water, which appeared ready to burst and overflow. *The Lord said never again will He flood the earth.*

Cush came up beside him, judging his father's fear; he placed a hand upon his shoulder. "It will subside, Father."

Ham lifted his chin and gazed across the desert plain between the Blue and White Nile. Gazelles sprinted to and fro. Palm and acacia trees grew thick in abundance. Rabbits peeked out at the newcomers from under shrubbery.

We were supposed to separate. Fill and replenish the earth. Ham realized now how much fear he felt; his brothers, Japheth and Shem, as well. They huddled together on the plains in Shinar like feeble old women.

Ham's second- and third-born sons drew up beside them. Ham waved a hand across the landscape. "Sennar. Our new home, though I suspect this plain may not hold all of us."

"Have we spread out far enough, Father?" Mizraim said.

"I hope so."

"Do not worry," Cush said. "Four of my sons have decided to cross the Arabian Peninsula. Nimrod will remain in Asshur."

"And Canaan—" Ham broke off in mid-sentence. "All will be well."

"We can follow the Red Sea southward, survey the land there, or northwest," Phut said.

"The north remains underwater," Mizraim said. "Else we would go that direction." Phut looked north. Mizraim pointed and said, "Where the River Nile flows upward." Phut nodded.

"In time," Ham said. "The mountainous highlands are sure to send enough mud down to make the land firm again." He sighed. *It looks like home. Feels like home. But I never imagined living so far apart from my brothers. I couldn't understand their speech if I did ever see them again. The Lord saw fit to confound our tongues. "Chestnut" ... I shall never hear my nickname called again. As the Hamite priest and patriarch, I say, Selah. God's will be done.* "Cush, you will remain here."

"As you wish, Father."

***

Nakhneith raised her short shift and scratched a mosquito bite. "Do you think he's really dying?"

"Nonsense," Horus said. He pushed his wiry body backward, then, swinging forward he let go of the tree limb and sailed to the next one. When his long skinny fingers gripped the limb, Horus let out a grunt of satisfaction. "Father Ham shall live forever. Just like Father Noah."

"Father Noah rested in his nine hundred and fiftieth summer," she said. The bark Horus held onto peeled away under his fingers. "Hor, you are going to fall … again."

"I think not. I am no mere human, you see." Bark slivers fell down and landed on Nakhneith's short, curly hair.

"Hor!" She brushed away the bark and shot him a frown. "Just because you have cheated death before doesn't make you more than human."

"Does it not?"

"No. Besides …" Horus lost his grip and fell to the ground with a thud. "Hor, you silly goose. Did I not warn you?"

"Yes," he mumbled into the sand. "It appears you were correct."

Nakhneith ran off to fetch Hor's mother.

Cush bent down and peeked inside his father's tent. Ham's chest rose and fell in even rhythm. He lay on a woven flax sheet. His chestnut brown skin showed few wrinkles, his once powerful body shrunk with age. Behind Cush, Mizraim whispered. "Does he still sleep?"

Cush ducked out of the tent. "Yes."

Mizraim paced around the tent. Phut sat atop a boulder with his head between his knees. Canaan spoke to his eldest son Sidon about the acquisition of cylinder seals, lapis lazuli, and silver.

Forever the merchant, Cush thought as he passed. *Father is dying, and they speak of a trade.*

We were supposed to separate, Ham remembered when he awakened. His eyes opened. *Did we not?*

"Cush!" Ham cried. "Did we not separate as the Lord our God commanded?"

Cush rushed inside his father's tent. "I am here, Father." He dropped to one knee at his father's side. Mizraim and his eldest son, Ludim, joined Cush in the tent. "We have done as the Lord commanded, Father. I am on the upper end of the river."

Should we have spread out more? Ham wondered.

"Mizraim." Ham cast bleary eyes at his second-born. "You were supposed to survey the land north of Cush."

"Indeed, Father. The moment the land firmed, we moved there. Do you not recall my Osiris leading the Anamin there at the first?"

And Canaan? Ham closed his eyes. *Yes, my youngest settled his sons, Sidon and Heth, along the Red Sea.* Ham turned his head to the side. He heard rain, waves crashing against the ark. Water... *What was underwater?*

Mizraim's scouts returned to Sennar to say the land remained underwater. When the mud descends from the mountains, the land will firm. And we will be in obedience to what the Lord our God said. Separate, said He. *Be fruitful and multiply.*

Cush, Mizraim, and Ludim stood and left the tent.

A mosquito haze hovered above the river. The afternoon skies mellowed into a yellow-orange. Nakhneith's arms swung as she sprinted on stubby legs toward the well where Isis, Horus' mother, was sure to be. She didn't mind. She was glad to see the clans reunited again. She didn't much like it when the clans separated, though Mother kept insisting she was too young to remember.

She would miss Horus when he returned to Kham. Horus and his daring antics. Yes, they were all together again, though for a sober reason. Father Ham is dying. She knew it. Even if none of the adults will admit so.

Nakhneith stopped short. No women surrounded the well. She ran to the fields where the cows grazed. No men, only young boys. They will be no help. They will ridicule cousin Horus for being in another accident. She wrinkled her nose. *Where are all the elders?* The Hamite clan banners waved to the far left. She took off in that direction.

Nakhneith saw a large purple cloth tied to a pole: the Canaanite banner. The banner of Cush, Nakhneith's great-grandfather, displayed a sparrow-hawk. Great-uncle Mizraim's portrayed a fierce falcon. Phut's banner depicted an elephant.

The adult men congregated outside Father Ham's tent. Nakhneith spotted Isis, off to the side with the other women. Nakhneith shuddered when she realized she'd have to pass cousin Set. She squeezed through bodies, crawled between a forest of black, brown, and tawny legs.

Nakhneith tiptoed to Isis and tugged at her frock. Isis glanced down at the child and sighed. Without a word, she took Nakhneith's hand and ran to where Horus lay.

Set's eyes followed them as they passed.

Ham awakened to the sound of raised voices.

"Father Ham should be buried in grand style …"

"Grandfather will never approve of what you are suggesting."

"Can you not stretch your mind a bit, cousin? Broaden your horizons."

"Father Ham would wish us to remain true to the Lord our God."

"What I suggest is not a departure from the ways of the Lord. It is merely to ensure our patriarch survives in the minds of his people."

"It is idolatry!"

"Would you rather our Ham be remembered as the father of Canaan—"

The Canaanites cried out as one. "Foul!"

Ham pictured in his head how his kin must be posturing themselves right now. Osiris would have his head cocked. Nimrod would stand with his feet apart, huge powerful hands on his waist, his head tilted in pride.

What angers Set? He was not even born when Father Noah issued the prophecy against Canaan. And being a grandson of Mizraim, he will not be affected by the curse. He will never serve Brother Shem's descendants. If Canaan can accept his fate ...

Ham closed his eyes and remembered. Father Noah stumbled out of his vineyards. His pride and joy. He spent most of his day in the vineyard, singing to the vines, checking their leaves for pests. That one memorable day, much to his wife's dismay, Noah again enjoyed the fruits of his labor.

His vision blurry, Noah managed to make out his tent up ahead. His sons—Shem, Ham, and Japheth—were erecting a new tent for Javan and his wife. The last one had become too small, as they were expecting a fourth child. The Lord commanded them to fill the earth. Be fruitful and multiply. *Just so, Lord*, Noah thought as his head continued to spin.

Another thought came to mind, something else the Lord had commanded. Noah couldn't grasp it at the moment. He focused his energy on making it to his tent without shaming himself in front of his clan; after all, he was priest and patriarch.

Noah disappeared inside.

Outside, Canaan put his tool down, turned to make sure no one watched, then crept toward his grandparents' tent.

Cursed be Canaan. A servant to Shem. Ham opened his eyes and felt anew the familiar pangs of regret. *What could I have done different?*

"Are you suggesting we place our ancestors in the place of God?"

"Blasphemy!"

"I am suggesting a memorial …"

Ham's eyelids fluttered. He heard shouting. He struggled to rise, but couldn't muster the strength at eight hundred twenty-five summers old.

"This is a departure, cousin, from the ways of the Lord."

Ham could not open his eyes. He felt drowned in slumber. He fought to stay alert. Stay alive. *I must arise. And see to these sons of mine. Idols? A memorial? Have they forgotten the abandoned tower in Babylon? This course will lead to our ruin. Idolatry. It will lead to chastising from the Lord. Lord God, I must arise. I am their priest and patriarch.*

And I am yours. Son, it is time to rest.

Ham let his muscles relax. A smile crept onto his face as the breath of life escaped.

Asenath

Annu
1994 BC

Poti-pherah, priest of Ra, had no appetite. He had drunk beer to break fast this dawn, but ate nothing. Now his stomach fluttered. Weariness had burdened him since daybreak. The discomfort meant one thing. Trouble brewed. He walked down the temple's stone steps, climbed into his waiting sedan chair and headed home.

Poti-pherah's two-storied villa sat on a broad street outside Annu proper. Shady trees surrounded the homes here, a beloved feature in any noble neighborhood. The priest craned his neck out of the vehicle, making sure the house still stood.

No fired had consumed it like the one at his neighbor's two doors down. A stray ember in the kitchen house had spread to the lord's great dining hall, then engulfed his wife's house before the neighbors managed to subdue the blaze.

A wall surrounded the front garden. Two baby birds splashed about in Poti-pherah's small pool. His daughter, Asenath, dressed in a simple white frock was kneeled in the garden. *Stubborn one. How many times must I inform the child that it is the duty of the gardener?*

***

Inside the royal palace at Itj-tawy, Neferenpret, Vizier –in-the-North, hastened to his duty. He strode down the palace corridor, sensing his ancestors' congratulations for keeping his countenance. Truly, Mother Nakhneith was speaking to

Fathers Ham and Cush about his composure. *For Horus'
decision is unheard of.* Now, outside the throne room, he let
his nostrils flare and slapped his double-kilted thighs with his
palms to prevent punching a palace wall. *Unimaginable.
How dare he?*

He rounded a corner, heading to the royal guest apartments.
When he stepped into The Blue apartment, the staff stiffened
and moved aside to let the vizier survey their handiwork.

Shaven and scrubbed clean, one might never guess the
Hebrew spent the last thirteen years incarcerated. He appeared every inch a nobleman: jeweled and in the finest
cotton robe the Black Land produced. Neferenpret gave a
curt nod of approval. Joseph slipped his feet into the papyrus
reed sandals and sat down to wait for his wife.

Outside, Neferenpret hailed a mule-driven cab, in no particular hurry to perform this errand. Once underneath the white
canopy and shielded from the populace's eyes, Neferenpret
exhaled his frustration. He was surprised to feel moisture
come to his eyes. He remembered Kheti's face when the
announcement came. *What did he feel? How will he tell his
family this news?*

*It is true none of us could interpret the dream. But why give
the foreigner such a lofty position? Would not a villa in the
country suffice?*

When Neferenpret arrived at the quay, he noticed the king's
man had followed him. Neferenpret stepped into the boat.
Glad now he did not stop and vent amongst his peers. He
wished to. Nothing would grant him better pleasure right
now than to curse the king's name while downing a beer. If
the royal bodyguard saw fit to trail him, then the king must

have feared that his decision would spark treason. A detour, however innocent, would appear suspicious.

A steady wind pushed the midsized vessel southward to Annu. Soon, Neferenpret entered the reception hall belonging to the high priest. Poti-pherah appeared. He noticed the cold fury in the Cushite's sharp eyes. The priest jerked his head to the left. "Come, join me on the roof."

Neferenpret followed the priest upstairs. The flat roof sported two obliqued wooden boards, allowing northern breezes to cool the family on the floor below. A chipped two-seater couch with cow's feet sat alone, covered with yellowed leaves from the palm tree above. The priest swept them onto the ground with his hand before taking a seat.

"What is it?"

"The Hebrew has found favor with the king. I am to bring him a wife."

"A lotus blossom? For an unwashed foreigner?"

"He is clean. Still a bit hairy, but presentable. The king will not relent on his promise; he fears the Hebrew's God."

"Speak plainly, Vizier. What is it the king wants from me?"

"Your daughter, Asenath."

"Absolutely not," Poti-pherah said, turning his head away.

"High Priest, consider what you say. The governor of Annu cannot intercede for you. At present, we are all of us subject to His Majesty."

"A foul match if I ever heard one, Vizier. My lovely Asenath coupled with this foreigner. It is undesirable. My daughter should marry an Anamim, a kinsman here in Annu."

"The king gave this Hebrew, Joseph, a position. One that far exceeds mine or yours, though we are the Black Land."

"He intends to grant a foreigner the position of Grand Vizier? And what of Kheti?"

"It is already done. He is out. I am commissioned, High Priest, to bring Asenath to the palace and present her this husband."

After breaking the news to his wife and daughter, Poti-pherah sat in his garden as long as he could. When he returned to the house, he still heard anguished cries from Asenath's room. Three women wailed: Asenath, his wife, and the household servant who wept while folding Asenath's frocks into a large wooden chest.

Asenath screamed at her father. "You would wish me to marry a sheepherder!"

"Daughter, be calm. I shall bear no disrespect. Our clan is ancient and highly esteemed. The king had to select a lotus blossom worthy of this Hebrew's deed. His knowledge will save the Black Land from famine."

Asenath slapped her ears with her palms, wishing to hear no more, hoping her father had misheard the vizier's plan. "I was reared for the nobility amongst the sons of Ham. Not a Shemite."

"I know that all too well, Asenath, but this marriage is ... It is the king's command, dearest. We must endure it."

Poti-pherah, Neferenpret, Asenath, and her body servant made the trip to Itj-tawy at Ra's rise. When the introductions were performed, Neferenpret made his excuses and left the now-married couple.

Weak from sobbing, Asenath dropped onto a couch. She raised her plaited head and stared at her new husband sitting on an old-fashioned campstool. Her eyes started from the top of his head and traveled down to his hairy toes.

I, a daughter of Ra, given to this blue-eyed foreigner. For one matter, I do not like his eyes. Hard to read. For another, he is still far too hairy.

Joseph, on the other hand, felt relief. He had feared receiving a wife who was perhaps a bit older than he would wish. The image of Potiphar's promiscuous wife came to his mind. The image had haunted him during his thirteen years in prison.

A plaited wig usually covered her gray, kinky hair. The red ocher she used to stain her cheeks appeared cracked, slipping between skin drawn with age. Her claim of rape, the reason for his incarceration, was absolutely ludicrous. In prison, he often amused himself by laughing out loud whenever her vision arose.

Here sits a proper lotus blossom. Young, brown inquisitive eyes stared at him. She did not smile upon introductions. She regarded him as if he were a blight splotch on a calf.

She leaned back on her arms and crossed her gold-sandaled feet. "I thought you sheepherders preferred our Canaanite brethren?"

Joseph cracked a smile. His uncle Esau took three Canaanites as wives. "It is truth; my people live amongst the Canaanites, but we are forbidden to intermarry."

"How flattering. Why do you abide in their land if they are so distasteful to you?"

"Canaan has been given to us by our God."

She sniffed. "How inconvenient for the Canaanites. Cannot your God find your people a land to call your own?"

Joseph rose. "Indeed, He is able. At present, we are a small nation and have no need for a lot of land. Besides, we are not populous enough to arm it."

He took a long deliberate look at the lavish furnishings. "Are you pleased, wife, with our dwellings? An apartment in the king's household is a great honor." He fingered an ornate rug hanging on the wall.

"Perhaps for a Hebrew used to dwelling in goatskin tents. Not for me. I much prefer my father's villa in Annu."

"If the king permits, I should like to return with you to your father's house, if nothing more than to meet with your family. Two brothers only? You were indeed fortunate; I have eleven brothers."

An inward pang pierced his heart; he fought it down and hoped for a change in his wife's expression.

At the same time, Asenath imagined her brothers' reaction to this husband; the scene the Hebrew would create brought a mischievous smile to her lips.

Joseph thought this a good sign and continued. "Maybe the king would allow us a home of our own. Would that not please you?"

"Perhaps."

Poti-pherah stood before the two solid wood doors, taking a moment to put his mind in good humor. Finally, he nodded assent to the chamberlain to announce his presence. The high priest entered the audience room and bowed before His Majesty. Amenenhat I studied the priest's face. "You are displeased, my lord?"

"Indeed yes, Your Majesty. I admit I had hoped for a far better match for my Asenath."

"You understand this Hebrew's God has done the Black Land a great service. I must give the man a position due him. Lest his God think us ungrateful for His wisdom."

"Indeed, I do understand, Your Majesty. And I have encouraged Asenath to befriend this Hebrew and bear him a son."

"I thank you, my lord, for your loyalty." He paused. "You will relay to me any discontented murmurings amongst the nobility. Since Kheti's departure and Zaphnath-Paaneah's promotion, I sense a change in posture. A profound displeasure, if you will."

Poti-pherah grimaced inwardly. *Zaphnath-Paaneah? A Khamite wife. A Khamite name. My, how precious this Joseph is.* Poti-pherah bowed. "Of course, Your Majesty."

Pharaoh flicked his hand in dismissal. He knew danger surrounded him. He, a Vizier before ascending the throne, felt it. He stared at the perspiration gleam on the high priest's shaven brown head, which remained lowered as he backed out of the room.

Accustomed to beef, a delicacy amongst the nobility, Joseph's expression did not mark surprise when he squatted down at the small stand and faced a platter of beef and leeks. He had eaten beef in Canaan on occasion. Oftentimes, the meat appeared in the home of Potiphar, captain of the guard.

An orange ray from Ra's descent illuminated the room. The family, with its new member, gathered for their first meal together. Asenath's two elder brothers and their wives had arrived this morning; they joined her parents and youngest sister for the evening meal.

Nine individuals, two people to a stand except for the youngest sister, sat on heavy rugs. Each stand piled with fresh dates, baked bread, and a roasted goose in addition to the beef and leeks.

Narrow-eyed stares came from both brothers, who managed to tear into the goose, pile their flat reed basket plates high with vegetables, and glare at Joseph at the same time. Their mother leaned forward and addressed Joseph. "You hail from Canaan, is that correct?"

"Yes, indeed, ma'am."

"Asenath tells me you are not allowed to form a household with Canaanite women. Is that correct?"

"Yes, ma'am. Due to their idolatrous practices."

"Idolatry meaning they do not revere your Yahweh," said the eldest brother.

"In short, yes."

"By the gods, Hebrew, how do you expect to prosper here in Kham? There is no temple here for your God."

"His name, son, is Zaphnath-Paaneah," Poti-pherah said.

"And his prosperity has been guaranteed by the Great House, with whom he has found favor."

"Yes, we have heard of this, Father. Shocking blow to Kheti and his kinsmen. I cannot imagine how they will endure it. But my question, more specifically, is how he thinks to endear himself to our people if he does not reverence our ancestors."

"And what, may I ask, is the difference between a daughter of Canaan and a daughter of Mizraim when neither worships the Hebrews' God."

"You ask a fair question, sir," Joseph said. "But I fear I cannot answer it. The wisdom Yahweh gave me for the king was at His good pleasure. I do, however, recall that the Canaanites sacrifice their children. An abominable practice your people would not think to do."

Both men grunted assent and focused on their meal.

Joseph did sympathize. How difficult for a priest of Ra to have a foreigner for a son-in-law. *What must his neighbors and peers think? Surely, Yahweh has a plan in all this.*

Joseph turned to his father-in-law. "May I ask, sir—you being a priest of Ra—how did the sun become a god and join your pantheon?"

The elder brother gasped and fell back onto the rug feigning despair. The youngest slapped his hand on the stand, and then put his face in his hands.

Asenath removed her drinking bowl filled with wine from underneath the table and drank deep. She longed to drown herself in the Nile. *'Tis a fate far more desirable than to be married to this ignorant foreigner.*

Poti-pherah, though, did not seem fazed. The gods, though important, were not the lifeline of Kham. That position belonged to the Nile and the Great House. Even some natives did not know what god from what animal to what village.

"Our ancestor, Ra, was one of the Black Land's earliest kings. He reigned for years here in Annu and saved the Black Land from a horrible fate. Do not fret over this ignorance, son. Many Khamites do not understand our gods, our ancestors, and how they came to be."

"My gratitude, sir. It would be dishonest if I allowed you to believe that I will embrace your gods. For I cannot. Yahweh is a jealous God. But I will make every effort to learn your people's history and embrace Kham as my own.

Asenath and Joseph were due to return to court in two sunrises. Earlier, Asenath had complained to her mother about the outdated furniture in the king's apartments, and persuaded her to do some shopping before returning to Itj-tawy.

"How did the sun become a god, indeed," Asenath sniffed. Her mother laughed out loud. "He calls it idolatry. He sees the sun god as a gross substitution for the real God, Yahweh."

They strolled along a narrow street entering the merchant area. Merchants, carpenters, and masons for hire all lived and worked down this street. Both women wore yellow dresses. Asenath's did not have the braces across her shoulders like her mother's, but an embroidered lotus flower border instead; the dress's narrowness kept it from slipping down.

They entered a one-story, mud-brick building where a craftsman made couches. "An ebony inlaid with ivory would be just the thing, Mother." They peered around the small showroom, where the merchant displayed two couches and a chair. He sat in the corner carving a chair. Wood shavings covered the floor and his feet.

"I am surprised at the Great House," her mother said, "coming from fashionable Waset and furnishing his palace so sparsely."

"As am I."

"Do you think the king will allow you to have your own home?"

"If Joseph asks. The king will not deny the blue-eyed creature a thing."

"Asenath, you really must call your husband by his proper name." Asenath snorted in response before her mother continued. "If you make that kind of slip-up in court, you will embarrass both your husband and family."

"Yes, mother." She sighed. "I daresay our family suffers from enough embarrassment with the Hebrew addition."

"It is not that bad, dearest. Even your father and brothers realize it is not, for all their grumbling. Your husband has the second-highest position in the land. That alone makes him a worthy partner, does it not?"

"Certainly. A bit more attention to his shaving would not come amiss."

Her mother laughed again. She instructed the craftsman to make a small staircase for the raised ebony couch, as well as a matching chair.

"Do not, my dear, become preoccupied with your husband's Hebrew blood. It is said our own ancestor, King Ra, had two Aramean daughters, and were they not Shemites as well?"

Asenath snorted. "A mere political alliance."

"Like your own union, daughter. Quit making those detestable noises and remember it as so."

***

The meeting would occur in Memphis. The older man arrived early. He waited a long time to plot this revenge. True, he may be on his estate in the afterlife before the plan was executed. No matter. He did not fear Osiris' judgment, for surely the king overstepped his boundary, time and again.

First, the Hebrew's promotion. The dissolution of several offices held by the oldest families. One nobleman in Goshen now lives surrounded by sheepherders. The king allowed his pet Hebrew to bring his kin to live in Kham. Seventy people. By the gods! Why do such a thing? True they are a small nation, but a nation nonetheless. And what if they multiply? What a horror for the Black Land to endure. Perhaps the gods will judge Amenenhat I as not Set king, instead of a Horus.

The man wore a striped narrow dress, reaching down to his bare feet. He forsook sandals on purpose. He wished his arrival and departure unheard as well as unnoticed. He leaned against the gnarled trunk of a fig tree. Ripe figs littered the ground. The man bent carefully and selected two not yet rotten. He wiped them on his garment then chewed slowly, waiting for darkness to descend.

The Nile Taxi

1440 BC

The scavenger kept his papyrus reed boat close to shore. He held a net to catch fish, and a long stick to poke around for objects. The sea, quiet and calm, gave no indication it had divided, allowing Hebrew slaves to walk its grounds unscathed. *Heresy.*

The wizened old man cackled to himself. *I have worked this sea forty summers, and it never did anything more than what it is doing now.* The married father of four made his living coasting up and down the Red Sea searching for valuables washed ashore.

Vultures have cried and circled for several sunrises now. *I wonder what it could mean? Everything seems still. It is true? Have we been dealt a mighty blow from the hand of the God of slaves?* The scavenger stretched his neck, but from where he coasted near Nekheb, he could not see far north enough to find any evidence of the rumors.

Two million Hebrews had crossed the Red Sea—had crossed the portion measuring a quarter to a half mile wide. They escaped Pharaoh's army into Edom, the land founded by its patriarch: Esau … Jacob's ruddy, hairy brother.

The scavenger snorted his disbelief again, all the time watching a black cloud of vultures in the sky. *I shall find great treasure today. Yesterday, I found an armband of a charioteer, kilts, which the wife mended, and two white headdresses.*

The scavenger prodded his stick into the water and struck a solid article. With his right hand, he kept the stick firmly stuck to the piece and grabbed the net, letting it unravel in the water. He found an opening in the piece, perhaps another armband. He got it.

Lifting it up, he saw a royal cartouche engraved on a solid gold armband. *Heavy piece this is. Maaktre Hatshepsut.*

The scavenger, a native of Kerma in Cush, did not much care for Kham's recent domination. All the same, this proves it. The Great House did suffer a blow. The sibling nations, Kham and Cush were humbled.

Hatshepsut, living forever! Has flown to heaven, and another stands in her place.

The scavenger edged the boat around toward home. He had found enough this day.

***

Coming in the opposite direction, up the Nile River, a well-crafted vessel moved at a steady clip. Its sail depicted a sparrow-hawk in an upper corner, a sign of Cushite nobility. The Cushite, indeed a descendant of Nakhneith, stood inside the boat, his chin tilted upward.

An observer might assume the man proud, arrogant even.

He merely compared the much revered temple of Karnak to his home temple, the great Gebel Barkal in Napata. He grunted his approval.

No, Alara had no excessive pride. His wife, sitting next to him, would tell anyone so. In fact, he'd be the first to admit that morbid fascination and duty brought him to Goshen. Furthermore, he knew where his prosperity came from: obedience to his father. Determined to join the Medjay,

Alara had trained in earnest. The moment he turned seven summers, he ran the entire length of the Dongola Reach with full barley sacks in his arms, aiming to strengthen them. A Cushite, especially a Medjay, had to be able to lift the heavy bow and fire it in precision.

His father, though, had said no. "You have two choices," his father said. "Join your brothers and me training horses for the nobility. Or attend school at Gebel Barkal and train as a scribe. Any fool can shoot and maim. You learn your glyphs, and you shall go far."

Alara compromised. He did both. First he attended temple school and worked as a scribe. He once drafted a letter for the king's son of Cush. Not that the administrator could not; he simply did not have the time.

Alara then served two summers in the Medjay, keeping Cush's borders free. Now at nineteen summers old, Alara had started his business venture. The Nile Taxi service transported passengers from Napata in Cush all the way to Avaris.

Alara knew the Nile's treacherous cataracts well, having lost two vessels to it. He used to drop his passengers off at Abydos, where an Egyptian-manned vessel would take the traveler farther north. No more. Alara built two sturdy vessels and opened a branch of the Nile Taxi in Waset.

He passed Waset, heading toward Avaris on an errand for his family. He found himself staring at a desolate, bruised Black Land. He heard the Nile had turned to blood, but it had faded before they set sail. He knew numerous heads of cattle were destroyed. Alara did not realize how bad the locusts had devastated the land; truly it did not look like the Black Land he knew.

"I have seen with my own eyes the desolation brought upon Kham. Why did not the Great House heed this Yahweh's words?" Alara said, staring at the locusts' damage. Bare acacias and once-stately palm trees appeared pathetic without their wide leaves.

"Kham will rebuild. Thutmosis will see to it," said his wife.

"No longer the falcon-in-the-nest. He shall head the Great House; for surely Hatshepsut has joined Osiris."

His wife gave an involuntary shudder. "If the sea delivers her now, it will be for a burial. Should we not turn back, Alara, before darkness arrives?" She cast nervous eyes about.

Alara gazed up at the fading sun. "Not quite. I wish to see the wreckage there." He pointed to lumps and debris on the shore. "You remember, wife, that my eldest brother served the Great House." She covered her mouth, embarrassed. "And see there, it appears the rescue team did indeed miss something."

His wife saw the arm first. The chariot with its broken wheels was deemed useless to repair. A man lay underneath the broken chariot, presumably dead. Alara made the short leap ashore. His wife eased herself out of the boat and onto the shore. She took tiny steps toward the still body. "Could not they have taken the man back to his home? His relatives may wish to give him a proper burial."

"His relatives believe he is under the sea with his comrades." Alara lifted the chariot and shoved it to the side. Underneath lay a lad; he appeared no more than twenty summers old. Caked blood formed a mound on one side of his head. "He breathes."

"Oh," said the wife. "Can you carry him to the vessel, Alara?"

"Of course." Alara kicked off his reed sandals. The wife grabbed them. He kneeled and hoisted the lad up, then tramped across the sand to where his ship and crew waited.

A priest with red-rimmed eyes met them at the temple entrance. His lids felt heavy from sleep deprivation, and an audible sigh escaped him at the sight of yet another plague victim. *How weary the Black Land is. How shall we recover? Whose idea was it to enslave the Hebrews at the first? That is what I wish to know. Did an ancestor seek to be avenged? A nobleman perhaps? What had the Hebrews done to spark that manner of vengeance?*

The priest turned and headed into the temple. Alara and a crewman followed, carrying Khaemweset into the stone-walled temple, down a flight of stairs into a tiny room. The priest cleared blank papyrus scrolls off a long table, and they laid the charioteer down. The lad's Amon-Ra necklace came apart; the pendant was lodged in the top of his kilt.

The priest retrieved it and held it up to the light. "A good omen. All is not lost in the Black Land."

"Toss it into the Nile," Khaemweset murmured. Alara, his crewman, and the priest stared at him aghast.

The priest leaned in. "You are delirious, lad. Amon-Ra, the hidden one, is king of the gods. You know not what you speak."

"I am in earnest, priest. I saw the hand of a God more powerful than Amon-Ra. I will continue to hold the ancestors of the Black Land in high esteem. But I can no longer worship them." The enormous loss of his comrades and monarch, made the charioteer's chest feel burdened with grief; he turned his head aside and wept.

The priest turned to Alara. "Go now. Leave him to my care. I shall restore his body, and when the Black Land recovers, it will restore his mind. He will once again embrace our gods."

"I doubt he'll ever worship his old gods again," Alara said to his wife as they readied to retire. "That lad witnessed all we have heard rumored. The sea parted and closed again on Pharaoh Hatshepsut and her forces."

The wife removed her wig and placed it on the stand. "Shall we return to Napata, and give your father the news straight?"

"Indeed. How should I speak? 'Father, your eldest son died of boils, inflicted upon him by the God of his slaves?' It is a ludicrous dialogue."

The wife lay on the couch in a plain green shift. She placed her head on the headrest and stared up at the ceiling. "Only speak the truth, husband. He knows about what happened in Kham. Tell him that his heir died of illness during the chaos."

They quieted. Crickets broke through the night's stillness. Silence, though, reigned inside his brother's well-furnished villa, now empty. The owner and family now deceased. The slaves all gone, led through the sea by their God and His servant Moses.

"I spoke to the charioteer," Alara's wife said. "I asked him why he still lives. Do you wish to hear what he said?"

"Truly." Alara loosened his kilt.

"Well then. He said that he called out to the Hebrews' God for mercy."

Alara held his soiled kilt up in midair. "And this God, Yahweh, He heard the cry of a man in pursuit of His people..."

"And saved him."

"What mercy."

"Yes. I have never heard such. Have you, husband?"

He stretched out on the couch beside her. "No. Nor I."

The Prophecy

712 BC

The bald prophet rose from his knees and removed his prayer shawl. He kept his eyes closed; contemplating the prophetic words Yahweh had placed into his spirit. Called at an early age, Isaiah's ministry proved an embarrassment to his prosperous family. *If my family knew how I am to serve our Lord now ...*

Like most prophets sent by God to His stiff-necked people, Isaiah faced ridicule and scorn; but the abuse now came from Judah. Israel was now gone, deported to Assyria.

Isaiah had prophesied the Lord's warnings to Judah. The tribes—Judah, Benjamin, and a few Levites—were in the midst of committing the same sins their northern brethren Israel had.

He spoke out about the soothsaying and idolatry. The sacred pillars and wooden images erected high hills and underneath green trees. The constant incense burning. His words, direct utterances from Yahweh, fell on dull ears and hard hearts.

Isaiah folded his prayer shawl and laid it on top of the mat. He placed a clean loincloth and frock on top of the shawl, then rolled the mat up and stuck it under his arm.

I hope the sons of Ham will not be so. For their sakes.

Tirhakah

712 – 701 BC

Through the choppy waters of the Nile's fourth cataract, at the far end of the Dongola Reach sat Napata, imperial capital of Cush. In the town's center, a stalwart castle with solid limestone turrets and wide balconies housed the royal family, a dynastic line founded by King Alara.

Khensa, Chief Wife of Pharaoh Piye, stood trembling at the palace's entrance. Her short-cropped hair was caved in lopsided from sleeping on her side. She drew the cloak tighter around her body. A crackle from a flickering torch broke the silence. Seconds passed before the long, lean frame of the high priest appeared.

He bowed. "Your Majesty."

"Come. The king's condition has worsened."

Asleep in his lion-headed bed, Prince Tirhakah awakened when he heard sandals against the stone floor hurry pass his chambers. The curtain covering his doorway fluttered. Tirhakah watched it through lowered lids. *What hour of the night is it?* He yawned and pulled the cotton sheet up to his small, narrow shoulders. On the floor, the prince's kitten, Aneksi growled low as he wrestled with his wooden toy mouse.

Moonlight seeped through the window matting. Tirhakah could see his wooden ball, crocodiles, and boats stacked in a heap, fulfilling his mother's wishes to clean his chamber.

Aneksi leaped onto the bed and licked Tirhakah's cheek. Tirhakah got out of bed and stretched. He ambled toward his hippopotamus couch, where he had thrown his kilt when he readied to retire. Then he remembered again that his mother, Abar, had ordered him to clean his chambers before bed.

This is why boys should never be made to clean their chambers. Surely, one cannot be expected to find something when it is in its rightful place.

Tirhakah ran his hand across the giraffe chair. Nothing. He turned around to his bed with the lion feet then remembered the chest at its foot. He opened the chest and found his kilts, folded sloppily, but not hanging off the furniture as usual.

Tirhakah wrapped a kilt around his waist then went to see what the matter was. Aneksi trotted after him, the wooden mouse between his jaws.

Now six summers old, Tirhakah's formal education would soon begin. He would learn to write, compute figures, and study literature. He would travel to Waset, where the priests at Karnak would oversee his education. Then there would be military training.

Tirhakah stuck his lips out at the thought of it. He didn't look forward to that. He wanted to be a priest at Gebel Barkal here in Napata. Or even a small temple in Kham.

What he did not wish for, and he dared not say it aloud, was to become king.

Tirhakah slipped past the servants and priests standing before King Piye's door. Queen Abar sat in a chair to the king's right. To the king's left, Queen Khensa stood murmuring quiet prayers.

Tirhakah marched to his father's side. "Father, what ails you? You must not fly to Osiris just yet. You have much to teach me."

Piye gave a slow smile. "Tirhakah, my little priest." Tirhakah ducked his head, embarrassed. "I am not leaving at this moment. My ka is still strong within me."

"Tirhakah," Abar said. "Come here and do not trouble your father. He needs his strength to fight the demons attacking his body." Tirhakah gave his father a short bow then backed up to his mother's side.

His uncle, Shabaka, co-ruler of Cush and Kham, came in and bowed low before his elder brother.

Piye whispered to him. "What is the news?"

"Iamani of Ashdod has arrived, bearing gifts. He seeks refuge. He is aware that Sargon wants him removed from power." He clasped his hands. "What should our response be? If we return him to Sargon too promptly, it would appear we fear the might of Asshur, Nabu, and Marduk."

"Iamani has no legitimate claim to the throne. And his appointment has angered Sargon. What benefit is it to us to befriend an imposter and enemy to Assyria?"

"None at all."

"Have a detachment take him to Nineveh. Gifts and all."

"I shall summon a scribe."

"Do not. Place this order under your seal. It shall be your first official act as king." Piye twisted a sparrow-hawk ring off his forefinger. He grunt with exertion, but leaned over and placed the ring on his brother's finger. "You are the mighty bull in Napata and Men-nefer. I leave you, brother, the lands of Ham."

Tirhakah watched his father and uncle's exchange. He sensed the tension and sorrow in the room, but did not understand its meaning. He thought it best to remain and hear the Chief Physician's diagnosis. He backed up farther, intending to be invisible, but a teary-eyed Abar sent him back to his room. "Go on with you. You shall hear of your father's progress when Ra rises."

"But—"

"No protests."

Tirhakah's shoulders slumped. He returned to his chambers, Aneksi following.

***

An indigo blue dawn spread across the land between the rivers Euphrates and Tigris. In Nineveh, on the Tigris' eastern bank, Mulisi and her husband, Ashur-dan, stepped out of their one-story home. They crossed the cooking area and opened their inn, The Shiny Pomegranate.

Inside, cedar chairs were stacked on top of square tables. Small red pomegranates were painted as a border around the dining room's wall.

To the left of the dining area, a short flight of stairs led to four guest rooms. Mulisi had insisted on numbering the doors with pomegranates. Ashur-dan thought it a bit much and told her so. She had laughed and tossed her naturally curly hair.

As a compromise, she gave each room an ensign on the background of a pomegranate. The first room depicted a one-horned ox, the auroch. The second room showed a lion. The third room showed an eagle in flight with a serpent in its mouth. The fourth room, many had commented on because of its oddity: a man holding a club.

Outside in the cooking area, Ashur-dan plucked and halved pigeons. Mulisi tossed the readied pigeons into a pot of boiling water. She always told people that she had been cooking since she was five summers old, though many doubted her claim because she could barely reach the cooking pot now at eight and twenty summers.

"A prophet is going to come, Ashur, mark my words."

Ashur-dan wiped bloodied hands on an apron, then he handed her a bowl of chopped onions and garlic. "Agreed, my Muli."

"Assyria has returned to her heathen ways. You can just imagine what is going on at the royal palace this evening. Imagine! Everything that Nineveh was almost destroyed over."

She closed her eyes in remembrance. *Another nation. Similar crimes.* She tossed the contents of the bowl into the pot. "Oh, how I wish I were alive during the time of Jonah the prophet."

"'Twas a horrible time, that. The skies turned dark during the day. A plague hit. People thought the gods disfavored them. They were ready to repent."

Mulisi turned to him and smirked. "Yes, but they did not know they managed to offend the Almighty God, now did they?"

"No. They did not. I doubt if many knew of His existence."

Mulisi hooted. "But they knew when Jonah came to town."

"What is not funny, my Muli, is the people have forgotten."

Mulisi sobered. She picked up a wooden spoon and stirred."I know. That's why I believe we are due for another prophet. I mean, what's the matter with Sargon, eh? Do we really need to do all this warring? Warmongers. That's what we are, Ashur. Everybody hates us."

"Agreed, my Muli. The Lord may soon judge Sargon and Assyria. Who is to say this time we deserve His mercy?"

"Right." She looked up and off into the distant. The sun peeked above the horizon. Hebrew servants carried buckets to the River Tigris, fetching water for their masters' baths. "It was mercy that spared us the last time."

***

A rooster crowed. Servants ran up wide stone stairs and outside. A brunette serving girl tidied her hair and smoothed out her frock. A few servants chewed on mint leaves to freshen their morning breaths. The stable hand gulped water down, then spewed out a green stream into the flowerbed.

The master waited in the courtyard. His legs crossed. Black eyes narrowed. A coiled horsewhip rested on his lap. He counted each slave as they assembled.

Two plump cooks, both with curly brown hair, rushed forward. They could be sisters. The master never ventured to find out. The slim, freckle-faced gardener arrived. Followed by the three maids: two blondes and a redhead; they looked at each other with wide eyes. The youngest maid still had a clump of green mint in the corner of her mouth.

Seven servants stood before him. A lad of fifteen summers old had disappeared. The number of missing slaves in the master's household had risen to five.

One of the cook's knees began to knock together. "Perhaps he has overslept, master. Shall I go and check?"

"No need, Rebecca. He is gone." The master gripped his horsewhip and rose. The maids burst out in sobs.

***

Sargon's fortress, Dur-Sharrukin, stood a few miles to Nineveh's north. Once completed, the city would have seven fortified gates, and a second fortified gate inside, strong enough to withstand an advancing army. At present, the fortress remained vulnerable enough to let a commoner walk through unquestioned.

This is exactly what the lad did. The eyes and ears of Marduk of Babylonia, the lad's youthful features suggested innocence. The ordinariness of his appearance caused no one to pay any particular attention to him. Fortunately he was not there to cause harm. All he wanted was information.

Inside the city's wall, he passed a ziggurat outside the king's palace. He skirted around the construction toward a terrace to the right, a temple of Nabu. He entered a courtyard, pausing when he saw a blur of silver to the left.

A female body, a royal female body from the looks of her, headed toward a wall of pillars. The lad removed himself from sight. This could be something useful. He slid behind potted palm trees.

She looked around the courtyard before taking off her silver sandals; then tiptoed behind the pillars, their meeting place. A person or persons could hide behind the wide pillars. The courtyard would be one of thirty. The water fountain muffled noise.

The lad watched as a man with a confident stride came into the courtyard, olive-skinned, strong aquiline nose, coal black hair, moustache, and beard. His profile resembled King Sargon. The man took a wide glance of the courtyard before disappearing behind the pillars.

He didn't walk like normal mortals. He strode. Sargon, king of Assyria, always strode to his horse. He strode to perform his duties in the temple of Nabu. Right now, he strode through the citadel gates, past two enormous bull-men statues. His gleaming black hair and blue embroidered cloak swayed with each stride.

Women wanted to touch him when they saw his stride. Touch his shoulder-length black hair that curled at the end. Touch his shimmering black moustache and beard.

Many wondered if Taliya, his wife, did not rub scented oil into his facial hair. Surely, she did something to get it to gleam so.

Sargon strode past the half-built ziggurat, heading toward the construction that would be his new palace. Eight dagger-men flanked the king, four on each side. Seven were burly, save for the long-legged, gaunt man on the left side. They all sported thick, black beards. The tall one wore his hair and beard plaited. Each carried a short sword and a dagger slipped into their leather skirts.

They walked erect in half-boots laced in front, careful not to imitate their sovereign's swagger.

The king and his entourage toured the fortress, checking its progress. Sargon strode around a completed courtyard with four large pillars in place.

The lad inched around a tree as Sargon's commander in chief, the *Tartan* ran into the courtyard trying to catch up with the royal party.

The lad bent down and crawled past the trees toward the pillars. He smirked when he heard a female's gasp. A male voice hissed silence. The lad swung a right and ran back toward the ziggurat.

Sargon lifted a hand, summoning his commander in chief forward. His forehead moist with perspiration, the *Tartan* bowed. "Your Majesty. Please pardon my tardiness."

"Ashdod needs to be disciplined. How soon can you get off to Canaan?"

"Will three to four sunrises suffice?"

"What delays you?""My Hebrew slaves, several have gone missing. This morning I administered chastisement."

The king laughed, a low rumble rising from his throat. "Where is this upstart, Iamani?"

"Seeking refuge in Musri and Cush."

"The king of Cush is in a hard to reach spot. Any chance the king knows of Iamani's rebellion? Perhaps he does not know Iamani displeases me."

"I shall make inquiries, Your Grace to make certain."

***

"By the gods, Yabu. You have reared a worthless female."
Yabu responded to her elder sister's criticism by shooting a
glance at her only child. Naqia, sixteen summers old, could
read, write, and discuss politics as well as any man. At this
moment, she shoved unleavened dough into a clay cylinder.
She tossed her hair back and looked up at her elders. Her
black eyes flashed then softened when she saw their fake
horrified expressions.

"Naqia, dearest, having bread for the meal is the point,"
Yabu said, jerking her head at the globs of dough on the
ground. "I know that you are anxious to escape, but take
care. You are not leaving until your chores are complete."

Yabu sifted coriander seeds. She picked out the firm ones
and dropped them into a clay bowl. "She is not worthless,
Lis. Women's work does not suit her."

"What else does she expect to do? I do hope you marry well,
niece, for you will certainly need a bread maker." Lis and
Yabu laughed.

Naqia tossed her mane of chestnut hair and smiled. "I intend
to, Aunt."

Naqia snatched the woven reed basket from the servant's
hand and ran barefooted toward the city's gates. She didn't
want to miss anything. True, her mother and aunt's humor
made the dreaded chores bearable, but they also slowed her
down. By her father's side is where she wished to be. Listening. Absorbing information. Interesting tidbits. Nothing to do
with bread baking or making pigeon stew.

Her father's routine was to leave his office and share a meal
with the elders at the city's gate. It kept him abreast of the

pulse of their village and Damascus as a whole. It had been Naqia's habit to bring her father his afternoon meal at the gate. She loved to listen to the old men debate politics.

Due to this arrangement—strange, yes, but now common to the men—Naqia knew of the doings in Babylon, where Marduk had appointed himself king. In Jerusalem, where the young and handsome King Hezekiah reigned for the past three summers. Also in Men-nefer, where the Cushite King Shabaka ruled the entire Nile Valley with fierce care.

Naqia knew where the seat of power really lay. In Assyria. In Nimrud to be precise, the military capital. Assyria would soon rule the world. If her aunt and mother thought that she would remain here in their village near Mount Hermon, they were mistaken. Naqia had plans. Plans that did not include her modest family at all.

Naqia slowed her pace down to a trot. When she passed the last row of mud-brick homes, she arrived at the city's gates. "Here is she. My little pomegranate," her father, Zakuta, said.

"Father, how many times have I told you that I am not a pomegranate?" She stood on her toes and kissed his deep olive cheek. "I am neither round nor red." Her father and his mealtime cronies laughed.

Naqia had inherited her father's long limbs; her skin was unblemished alabaster and her waist-length locks possessed natural red highlights. She had deep brown eyes that appeared black when she was angry or frustrated. Now that she was where she wished to be, at her father's side, her eyes were brown and merry.

"You will always be my Pomie," her father said, taking the basket from her and sifting through its contents.

Menki, whose long white beard reached the ground, nudged Zakuta with his wooden cane. "Now, my friend, do you regret raising this child as a male? What do you intend for her now? She is too smart to marry," he said, cackling.

Zakuta shrugged. "What choice did I have? The gods denied me a son. I had to pour everything into her—she will in turn do her duty and give me lots of grandsons, right, Pomie?"

"As you say, Father."

"Speaking of grandsons," Zakuta pointed to a baby-faced lad. "Menki's grandson, Damqi has returned from Nimrud."

Naqia spun on her heels toward him. "Is that so? You have been to Nimrud, seat of the great Sargon? Why ever did you return?"

"It is complete." He waited for her to ask what was complete, but he didn't realize how informed the mayor's daughter was.

"Dur-Sharrukin is complete? Are you certain?" Naqia's eyes drank him in. This man has been to Nimrud. She wanted to reach out and touch him. She wanted to feel his experience. *Did he see the great Sargon? How many wives does the king have? Is he in need of another?*

"Well, almost." He blushed. "I was part of the work force for the last ten summers. Ten full summers it took to build. Two hundred rooms. Thirty courtyards …"

Zakuta chuckled at his daughter. It took much to impress her … but look at her now. Her eyes widened and she was still; it looked as if she had stopped breathing.

"There are seven fortified gates," the lad continued.

Naqia interrupted him. "What kind of celebrations will mark its completion? Days of feasting, I am sure."

"At the end of the plowing season, there are to be days of feasting. Dur-Sharrukin shall be inaugurated with a grand time. Dignitaries from Kham, Babylon … everyone will be there."

And so shall I. Naqia tuned him out. *I have to get there. I will get there. I must convince father and mother that a holiday is due us. They will return home, and I will stay.*

Zakuta saw his daughter's determined look and knew what was in store. *She would start with a polite, seemingly innocent request, presenting evidence that would be hard to refute. And if she was turned down. And she will be turned down. They simply could not afford such a journey. She will throw a tantrum and sulk for days.*

"Pomie?" Naqia's head whipped toward her father. "It is time you headed back. Your mother will chide me for keeping you from your afternoon chores. Away with you now. If there is more news, I will share it with you later."

Naqia curtsied to the men and left. When she was out of earshot, Menki said. "I think that your Pomie wishes to be at Dur-Sharrukin for its inauguration."

"My Pomie wishes to live at Dur-Sharrukin."

"Will she attend?"

"Not unless her husband takes her."

"When is she to wed?"

"At harvest time."

                        ***

A giraffe stretched its neck to the tree and munched at the leaves. The animal had been wandering into the front yard of the governor's palace in Kanad since the previous summer. Prince Khaliut stood in the palace's foyer with a papyrus sheet in hand, watching the animal. A white headdress covered the prince's shaven head, and a white linen kilt wrapped around his waist. Besides his reed sandals, he wore gold arm bracelets and a choker from turquoise beads.

Kanad, a small province in Cush where Khaliut governed, sat close to the royal palace in Napata. Indeed, Khaliut could walk to the country's capital if the mood suited him. He didn't wish to go. He didn't even want to read this directive, because it had the royal seal on it, and he knew whom it was from.

"Governor, shall I send a reply," the royal courier said.

"No. I shall answer Shabataka in person." Khaliut watched a bird land on a limb of an acacia tree and survey its surroundings.

"As you wish, my lord." The courier bowed and ran off.

Khaliut could not avoid it any longer. He looked down at the directive, which read: "I have a job for you."

At the royal palace in Napata, Crown Prince Shabataka rolled out of bed. The prince walked outside to the furnished balcony and sat down to break fast in the nude. His manservant was placing barley cakes and beer before him when the chamberlain announced his older brother's arrival.

"Prince Khaliut, Governor of Kanad, firstborn of King Piye, living forever!"

Shabataka ignored the announcement. He munched on a barley cake and watched afternoon life in the capital. Men rode past the palace atop elephants and donkeys. Women strolled by with children on their backs and children at their feet. Merchants rollicked along in ox-driven carts, taking produce to sell at market.

Khaliut walked into the chamber, grabbed a kilt spread out on the couch, and headed outside where he dropped the kilt onto Shabataka's lap. He sat down opposite him.

"You walked here, did you not?" Shabataka said.

"Yes, what of it?" Khaliut accepted beer from the manservant.

"You took your time, which tells me that you did not wish to come."

"I doubted you would be awake at this time of day."

Shabataka barked a laugh. Both men shared their father's round face, high cheekbones, and penetrating eyes. Khaliut, Piye's first son by Queen Khensa, inherited her small, aquiline nose. Shabataka, second son of Piye, was born to the former chief wife, Queen Tabiry.

"What job do you have for me?" Khaliut said.

"I need you in Assyria," Shabataka said, gauging his brother's reaction.

"You need me there, or the king does?"

"Same difference, is it not? I operate in the interests of Cush and Kham."

"What does the king wish me to do?"

"What always needs to be done in Assyria? Observe. Listen. Report any relevant information."

"Royal brother, King Sargon and our uncle are allies. I do not wish to undermine their friendship by communicating any mistrust."

"Then you will have to be discreet. Is that not the nature of your job as a royal reporter?"

"A position, that you well know, our father had me relinquish when he took the throne in Kham."

"Our father has soared to the heavens, and I am to succeed our royal uncle in his place. Are you to serve me in the interests of Cush and Kham, or not?"

Khaliut drained his beer. He stood and bowed.

"May the blessings of Amon-Ra be upon you," Shabataka called after him.

Khaliut walked out without acknowledging the "blessing." He didn't leave the palace, but sought out his mother. He greeted Queen Abar en route then endured a snub by Shaba-taka's mother, Queen Tabiry in the corridor.

Khaliut strolled outside the palace, up a short flight of stairs to a courtyard. There, dressed in a straight gold frock in bare feet, his mother Khensa picked flowers. Her close-cropped hair showed gray streaks, but Piye's sister and chief wife aged well. Her dark brown skin, mildly wrinkled, did not betray the fifty inundations she'd witnessed.

"Khaliut, what brings you here this day? Surely, you have not come to see your old mother."

"Old, perhaps. But still beautiful." He pressed his forehead to hers. "And you certainly look better than Tabiry; she just waddled past me." Khensa chuckled and gave her son a playful pinch on his arm. Khaliut sobered. "Shabataka has given me another assignment."

A distressed look crossed her face. "Oh, I do hope it is not like the last one. Encouraging that rebel Iamani—it is a wonder Assyria has forgiven us."

"Indeed. Which is why I need to see if Shabaka approves of this endeavor."

"Shabataka … He is Tabiry's own son. He fashions himself as king of Cush already."

"He is not even co-regent. I do wish my royal uncle made his home in Napata like Father had."

"What will he have you do this time?"

"Go to Assyria. Observe Sargon."

"And if you are found out to be observing Sargon, it will strain relations between us."

"Indeed."

The queen offered her arm to Khaliut. He looped his arm into hers and walked. "Try and delay your departure. I shall make a few inquiries."

**

Mulisi stood in the inn's doorway and watched them approach. She wrung her hands. *Surely, they do not mean to come here. So many.* Twenty Cushite soldiers wearing ivory necklaces and knee-length kilts marched toward the inn. Bare arms in black and brown shone with perspiration.

Their tattooed forearms grasped spears. A man bound in shackles and fetters dragged his feet in their midst. The captive's long black hair covered his eyes, patches of hair were missing from his moustache and tangled beard.

Mulisi rose on her toes' tips, lowered and looked back inside the inn to see if Ashur-dan had returned. She stood on her toes again and wrung her hands. The Cushite commander, attired in a leopard-skin cape, made a sharp left, leading his troops and their captive into the inn. Mulisi backed out of the way, allowing them entry.

She greeted them in Aramaic, certain they did not understand. Yet the commander returned her greeting in the same, requesting food and drink for his men.

The oldest patrons, Tenti and Justi, quit their arguing for the moment. Tenti held his game piece in midair, gaping at the guests. Justi stopped his words in midsentence. The Cushite commander handed Mulisi his goatskin.

Without a word, she hurried to the well in the courtyard to refill it with water. When she returned, the men had taken seats, leaving their captive standing propped against the wall. Mulisi ran into the back again to fetch food, ignoring questions that Justi and Tenti fired her way.

"Wee one, what are those Hamites about? Who's the rough-looking fellow with them?"

Mulisi exhaled relief when Ashur-dan entered the dining area. He laid his burden on the counter and sauntered toward the Cushite commander.

Mulisi came back with fresh dates, gourds of coconut milk, and cucumbers. While she ran about, Ashur-dan kept a steady conversation with the commander, even pouring him the inn's best date-palm wine. After the guards ate their fill, they allowed their captive some bread and water.

Mulisi rounded the counter, barely missing the sharp wooden edges. "Slow down, wee one, before you run into something," Tenti cackled.

Finally, the commander stood and handed Ashur-dan two silver pieces. When the contingent stood at attention and marched out, Mulisi dropped into a chair. Ashur-dan saw them out. When he returned to the dining room he said. "That captive was the Javanite, Iamani. They are taking him to Sargon, for he escaped to Napata seeking refuge."

"And Piye ordered him here? Surely Sargon will slay him."

"Piye has soared to the heavens, my Muli. His brother, King Shabaka, reigns in his place. This was a wise move on his part, I am thinking."

Mulisi rubbed a throbbing foot. "Hmm."

***

Naqia kneeled down and added a folded frock to a traveling basket. "For you, my lady." She turned to see her cousin, Aki, standing in her doorway holding a dead pigeon by its feet. *How dare he? Does he think he can come to my room whenever he wishes?*

"Thank you, cousin. Please give it to one of the servants."

"You know that I cannot. It is your chore to make the evening meal." He grinned, showing uneven yellowed teeth.

"Why are you packing? Going somewhere? Dur-Sharrukin, perhaps?" he laughed.

"Will you please leave my chamber and take that outside where it belongs."

"You realize that we will not have as many servants as you do now."

"We?"

"Have you not been told? We are to marry at harvest time." He cocked his head, staring at her profile.

Her nostrils flared. "Do not be so sure of yourself, Aki. In the end, I shall marry whomever I please. My father would not wish me unhappy."

"Your father has spoiled you. He dotes upon you as if you were a male child. It has been agreed that I am the best choice to tame you."

Naqia stood and crossed the room; she snatched the pigeon from his hand and moved past him.

"Mother, what are your objections to taking a holiday? Father works hard—"

"Naqia, I am your mother. I carried you, fed you, and reared you. I know what you want. We are not going to Asshur. We will not be attending the opening of Dur-Sharrukin. Your father has a town to run. It is simply out of the question."

Naqia ripped the pigeon's feathers out with a frown on her face. Her aunt Lis walked past and made a sad face. "Poor bird."

"It is dead, aunt."

"For certain," she said, strolling inside the house.

Damqi, seventeen summers old, told everyone who would listen that Naqia, the village beauty, found him special. She had gazed into his eyes as if in a trance. She had asked him questions about his work in Nimrud. If that was not the making of a coupling, then Damqi did not know what was.

Tall and stout with chubby cheeks, Damqi was the youngest child. His mother, a delicate woman whose health declined after birthing twelve children, listened aghast at his account.

"Damqi, get from under your mother's frock," his father said, walking passed the cooking area.

"I thought that I will help Mother clean, Father. She is feeling poorly."

His father shooed him away. Damqi hurried outside, his expression brightened when he noticed his friend Aki approaching. "Damqi, you look pale, my friend."

"Aye, Father has once again accused me of being a female."

Aki laughed heartily and slapped his friend on the back. "Come with me for a moment. I shall play a joke on my cousin. Just follow my lead." Damqi nodded, hoping Aki's prank wouldn't get him into more trouble.

As they approached, Naqia remained on her knees, still plucking the pigeon.

"Cousin," Aki said. "Can you not guess? Damqi here is returning to Assyria, shortly? Isn't that right, Damqi?"

"Uh, yes. Better jobs there. Ships to build …" Two spots of red crept upon his cheeks. He remembered their earlier exchange and relaxed. "I have experience as a builder, my lady. There is much work in Nineveh, I am told."

Naqia let the pigeon fall to the ground. She stood and wiped her hands on her frock.

Aki watched with an impish grin. She will never get to Nineveh. It is her duty to remain here and marry me. This prank serves as her punishment for not being keen on the idea. He was a great match; she would be smart to recognize the fact.

"When are you leaving, Damqi?" Naqia said.

"After the harvest is in."

Aki grinned and held back a snicker. Naqia arched a brow at him before returning her attention to the red-faced Damqi. "Do you need a help mate?"

Damqi's jaw dropped open.

***

"Innkeeper!" The voice bellowed from inside the inn.

Outside in the courtyard, Ashur-dan and Mulisi shared a nervous look. He took her hand and squeezed it before going inside. Armed bodyguards crammed his dining room. Crown Prince Sennacherib stood in their midst. "There you are."

Ashur-dan bowed. "Pardon, Your Majesty. We have had a slow day."

"I heard that your establishment makes the best food in town. Better than the cooks hired for Dur-Sharrukin."

"I am honored to hear so, great Prince."

"I would wish a sample of your fare. If I care for it, I shall return to your inn. What do you have prepared for me?"

Ashur-dan ignored the prince's presumption. "I have rolled grape leaves with currants, and wheat soup made with fennel. And my wife is preparing a pigeon stew for tomorrow."

"Prepare me something to take with. Tomorrow, once I have sobered, I shall try your stew."

"Good day, Your Majesty," Mulisi said, bouncing into the dining room. She came to stand right above the prince's waist. "Welcome to the Shiny Pomegranate. What can we get for you? Grape leaves did you say?"

"Good day, madam. Your husband shall fetch me a sample of your cooking."

"A sample? We don't do samples, my lord, but we will make an exception this one time. Tomorrow you must be prepared to pay for my pigeon stew, for it will be worth the price, if I say so myself," she beamed.

Sennacherib took a full step back then stared down at the petite brunette. Slowly, he said, "As you say, madam." He turned to his bodyguards with a raised brow. They slapped their armored knees and roared with laughter.

***

He had deliberated long enough: stay and keep others safe, or flee. The latter would put his tribesmen in harm. Up to now, the decision had been simple. But more and more tribesmen had risked their lives for freedom. Why shouldn't he?

Hugging a woven basket full of fresh watercress, the gardener walked at a brisk clip off his master's estate in Habor near the River Gozan. A high-prow boat sailed past him on the Euphrates River. He passed reed huts home to fishermen and took a left entering town.

He longed to look behind him, to see if anyone followed. Maybe another kinsman chose this time to escape as well. He resisted the urge. It would appear suspicious. Did his pace seem out of the ordinary?

He saw the inn up ahead. *Freedom. Please, Yahweh. And I know I haven't prayed to You before. But You are the God of my fathers, Abraham, Isaac, and Jacob. But I am a slave in the land where the only god is Asshur.*

Two pomegranate shrubs flanked the inn's entrance. The gardener kept his pace steady, intending to veer toward the inn as if it were an afterthought.

His enthusiasm waned. His eyes clouded. Coming outside from the inn were several Assyrian guards, then a young nobleman. At least, he dressed as a nobleman in an embroidered robe, wearing a small conical hat. He could be royalty.

I cannot have gotten this far from the master and risk detection. A man, the proprietor perhaps, stepped to the doorway to see the nobleman off. The gardener paused deliberately, made a sudden swerve to his right and approached the inn.

"Good sir, I am told your inn makes the best watercress stew. Would you care to purchase a bushel from my master's crop?"

Ashur-dan gazed into the man's eyes and sensed his calm desperation. "I have a supplier, sir, but let me look at your merchandise. What is your name?"

"I am Joshua ben Solomon."

Ashur-dan picked through the bundles of watercress, checking the leaves for insect damage. He watched the scene before him. Crown Prince Sennacherib stood between his chariot and one belonging to a noble who had pulled up alongside.

The gardener peered into the inn, hoping to see a glimmer of freedom. He knew this to be the place the young lad went to before disappearing. He had described the overgrown pomegranate shrubs. Joshua endured his master's whipping for not telling of this location.

Inside, oil lamps were lit. Patrons drank beer through tubes. Some dined, probably feasting on the pigeon stew that he'd heard the inn made so well. Two older men, sitting near the brazier, played a board game, cackling loud and shaking their fists at each other.

Joshua imagined himself inside, his long legs stretched out before the brazier. His sole care? The state of his crops. Not whether or not he would be whipped this evening. He longed to inch past the innkeeper. He struggled to stay put. *Remain calm. What if the lad got it wrong? What if this was not the place? What if he arrived here, only to be arrested and impaled for trying to escape?*

Furthermore, this innkeeper can well work for the royal family. Is that not Prince Sennacherib right there? The gardener's face flushed. He imagined perspiration beads on his forehead.

"Are you well, lad?"

The gardener's mind raced. *Say no, perhaps he would usher me inside. Provide me with a beer to refresh myself. Say yes, and if it is the wrong inn, then I will get in unnecessary trouble.* "I am well, sir."

"Tell me, Joshua, what banner did your people travel under?"

A puzzled expression crossed his face. He was a Hebrew, yes. An Israelite, that much he knew. But their people had not traveled under banners for quite some time. *What manner of question is this? A trick? It certainly isn't a question for a lad raised in Sargon's Assyria. Perhaps my grandfather would know. He remembered the old ways of our people. Abraham. Moses. Aaron and the golden calf. Wait ...*

Ashur-dan noticed a spark of recognition in the man's eyes.

"An ox, sir. My people traveled under the ox banner."

"You look quite unwell, Joshua. Come in and lie down."

The gardener felt like jumping for joy.

"Hail, *Tartan*. From where do you come? Should you not be on your way to Canaan?" Prince Sennacherib called out to his father's commander in chief.

Joshua reached for the basket. Ashur-dan understood. He fished through his pocket for a piece of silver, handed it to the gardener and removed the watercress from the basket. The gardener's hand trembled, but he took the silver and gave a short bow.

He turned and faced his master. "Excellent timing, master." He bowed and gave the stern-faced Tartan the silver. "I managed to empty the barn this day of the last of the watercress. You needn't worry that cook will prepare you any more meals out of watercress," he added with a bright smile. He whistled as walked back to the villa.

Inwardly, he trembled. But at least he knew this was the right place. *Soon, maybe tomorrow, the master will be off warring. And I, Joshua, will not be here upon his return. If he returns.*

Temple Karnak
Waset

A wadded piece of papyri, moistened by spit, flew through the air and landed on the lowered shaven head of the priest. He pretended to not feel it. Keeping his head bent over his wooden tablet, he used his gnarled fingers to search for the next passage in his lecture.

The room remained quiet. A breeze blew off the Nile River and in through the pillars, separating the lesson room from the courtyard.

Another piece of papyri, bigger than the last, soared then bounced off the priest's head. This time Tjanefer raised his head and cast watery eyes at his pupils. The boys sat in a semicircle, cross-legged, each with a wood tablet on his lap and a reed pen in hand. Their facial expressions remained stern. No laughter appeared in any of their dirt brown eyes. They ranged in age from six to ten summers old, all sons of nobility.

Tjanefer's glance settled on whom he suspected was the culprit: Tirhakah. Always Tirhakah. The prince was a good student, but mischievous. Tjanefer had taught young boys for countless inundations. Was he intimidated by the young nobles in his classroom? Certainly not. He had instructed the present king, Shabaka, as a lad.

Tjanefer lowered his head and rasped. "A boy's ears are on his back; he hears better when he is beaten." The priest raised his eyes to Tirhakah. The prince's hand was raised in midair, armed with another wad. "And His Majesty has given me permission to ensure that all hear, and hear me well."

Tirhakah lowered his hand; his almond-shaped eyes danced with amusement. The lesson room erupted with laughter.

***

Hattusilis, Chief of Police, steered his donkey up the narrow winding road, pass lofty palms and tamarisk trees that shielded the noble-class villas. He puffed his chubby cheeks out, something he often did when perplexed. He had been in law enforcement for the last fifteen summers, having taken the post from his late father. Hattusilis felt out of his element here. He had no idea who to contact about this.

Or whether or not he should contact anyone at all.

Hattusilis stopped in front of a vine-covered villa with tiny white flowers in full bloom. He lifted one stubby leg up and slid off the donkey's back. He wrapped the donkey's lead around a tree trunk. He straightened his kilt before going inside the home of Pabasa, High Priest of Amon.

Pabasa poured goat milk onto his barley porridge. Hattusilis gave a curt nod. "High Priest." The priest wore a large ring on his right index finger, crafted in the form of an ibis. He hadn't put on his traditional panther skin, but broke fast in a common white kilt.

"Have you made contact with this person?"

He already knows? Hattusilis tore his stare away from the high priest's neck. Certain the priest's necklace was crafted in solid gold. "I have, sir. He seems harmless. All he does it utter harsh words against Kham."

"Naked?"

"Yes, sir. He is naked."

"Keep an eye on him for now."

"Should you not care to hear what he has to say, High Priest?"

"No, I shall not care to hear what he has to say. Just keep an eye on him for now. If he becomes troublesome, I shall alert the vizier."

Red spots broke out on Hattusilis' amber cheeks. He felt silly now. Maybe he should not have brought the naked stranger to the high priest's attention. *True, he hadn't done any real harm. It is what he says that is alarming.*

The Cushites and Khamites will be taken into captivity. Naked. With their buttocks exposed. Should not someone report this to the Great House? Perhaps I should have gone to the palace. The king may be interested to know that calamity is prophesied to befall the land of Ham.

Pabasa watched the policeman mentally wrestle, assured that he knew what the man thought to do. *But it will not do. He will not look a fool by going to the king with the vivid imagination of an unwashed foreigner.* Pabasa muttered a good day to the chief and returned his attention to his porridge.

Outside, Hattusilis was untying the donkey when it occurred to him. *There is something to be said about the high priest's manners. He had not bothered to offer the Chief of Police a cup of beer.*

***

With both hands clasped behind his back, Tirhakah rested his shaven head against the limestone wall. His feet were clad in papyrus sandals with upturned toes, crossed at the ankles. He waited outside the lesson room for his aunt to finish speaking with Tjanefer. When his aunt Tabakenamon had come to fetch him from school, the priest requested a word with her.

Tirhakah turned to his right to look outside, where the afternoon faded. His eyes returned to the white sheet covering the lesson door. He could see the outline of their bodies. The bare-chested priest stood stooped, his fingers and toes gnarled.

His aunt's turquoise ankle-length gown, and her small feet clad in silver sandals. Her hair did not frame her head in the style most Cushite women wore. Aunt Tabby grew up here in Ineb-nedj and styled her hair in Khamite fashion; she wore a long plaited wig with a silver and turquoise diadem on top. Her head inclined toward the priest, soaking up his every word about Tirhakah.

They spoke in hushed tones, as if his bad behavior was unknown in Ineb-nedj or Napata. They walked to the entry-way, still speaking. His aunt nodded her understanding. "I will send word to Abar." Abar, Tirhakah's mother resided in Napata, where most of the royal family stayed. "Meanwhile, I shall have a word with his uncle."

Nice. Tirhakah narrowed his eyes at the priest. *Now I will not be able to go hunting with Harey.*

Tjanefer and Tabakenamon came to stand before the lad. Prince Tirhakah straightened out of respect.

When his round-faced aunt spoke, Tirhakah lowered his head. "Tirhakah you are now hereby under punishment. You will not go hunting with your cousin Harekmakt. Tjanefer has been most kind as to spare you punishment for past deeds, but I will not be so. And neither will your uncle when he hears of your behavior. If your father were alive, you would never get away with this performance in school." She reached out a jeweled hand and laid it on his head. "Come along."

Tirhakah made his apologies to Tjanefer. He followed his aunt, the queen, Chief Wife of King Shabaka, out of the temple.

"Magnificent," said King Neferkare Shabaka. He smoothed out the leather roll of the text. "It dates back to the Old Kingdom, does it not?"

"Yes, Your Majesty. Designed to aid the priests in reenacting the story of Horus and Set," Pabasa said.

Shabaka leaned over the text, his hands grasping the edges of the table. He read for a moment. "'Philosophy of a Mennefer Priest.' High Priest, find me a fine piece of granite. We will transcribe this text into stone, where it will remain for eternity."

"Very good, Your Majesty."

Queen Tabakenamon came into the room and whispered into her husband's ear. Right outside the door, Prince Tirhakah stood with his hands clasped behind his back.

"Tirhakah!"

***

Mulisi entered the dining area carrying fresh palm fronds; she dropped them on the wood counter. Her feet and calves ached. Her fingernails reeked from peeling onions and garlic. She removed the dirty placemat fronds at each table, washed the tables clean and dry then went around placing the new palm fronds.

She narrowed her eyes at the last two patrons, knowing she couldn't close the inn until they tottered off for the evening. She took the oil lamps into the back area to pour fresh olive oil into them.

Tenti and Justi, both widowers, both regular guests, bent across the table in concentration. They sat at the same table next to the brazier every day, sharing a game board and a goatskin of date-palm wine between them.

Mulisi had purchased the game board for all her patrons. The two elders, though, seemed to think it theirs, fussing at patrons whenever they sat at their table, or dared to move a stone on their board.

"You cheat!"

"Bah."

Mulisi retrieved the inn's potshards and sat down at a table. Her feet dangled above the swept ground floor. She read through Ashur-dan's duties. *Need more cucumbers and leeks. Build a second clay oven. Trim the pomegranate bushes in front. Pay the informant about the news he provided on Sargon's next move. Bring in the barley harvest.*

She sorted through the potshards; some lists had entries on them relating to nothing concerning the inn. Perhaps I should learn to keep better records, like my husband.

Tenti thrust an arthritic fist in his companion's direction. "You are a goat's bladder, you are. Put that stone back."

"Make me. Sore loser."

"That's it," Mulisi said, dropping her reed pen. "The two of you go home before your servants come to fetch you."

"What servants?" said Tenti, the one Mulisi likened to a rat. His beady brown eyes, set in a narrow head seemed to twitch about involuntarily. The remaining white wisps of hair on his head stood straight up. "Mine disappeared after the wife died. This is why I come here every day to be served by you, tiny woman."

Mulisi hopped off the chair and marched on swollen feet toward them.

"Now look what you have done," Justi said. His bald head showed dark spots. "She will throw us out on our backsides."

The men stood in slow motion. Mulisi slid a palm frond from underneath the lamp on their table and made a swipe toward Tenti with it. "Out, the two of you."

Justi raised a liver-spotted hand. "See you tomorrow, wee one." They cackled as they exited.

Mulisi dropped into Tenti's seat, looking down at the game board painted in red paste and lapis lazuli. The stones would remain in the position of their last play. The two widowers, true to their word, would return after sunrise to break fast and resume their game.

Ashur-dan returned with the cooking pots washed clean.

Dare I document events that led us to Assyria? Ashur-dan would say no. "What if someone found your writings?" he'd say. *True enough. It is best to keep to myself my notes of the comings and goings at the inn. For now.*

But, oh, what wondrous news! Imagine. After all these summers, they have been found. Alive at that. Ashur-dan accuses me of being driven. He's certain my determination will get us both flayed. But once we're successful—and we are oh so close—then we can leave Assyria forever.

It is worth it, is it not?

A knock sounded on the inn's door. Mulisi watched Ashur-dan come forward.

"Sorry to disturb you at this hour, sir. My name is Hoshea. I've spent the entire day trying to sell the last of my master's pomegranate harvest. I hoped that your fine inn would relieve me of a few."

"Good evening to you. I am Ashur-dan, proprietor. Hoshea, did you say? I once had a slave by the same name. From where do you come?"

"Shiloh." Hoshea leaned in and whispered. "I hear a man can gain a new life from savoring your meals."

"I have no idea what you mean by that, sir. But if it is praise you mean to offer, it must go to my wife, Mulisi. As it is, we have had a fair pomegranate harvest." He gestured toward the shrubs flanking the inn. "Do not let these meager bushes fool you. With regret, I must pass on your offer. Bid your master my good wishes, sir."

The man did not offer a bow, or a departing word, but hurried away. Ashur-dan stared after him, taking in the man's curly black hair, medium height, and stick-thin legs. He closed the door.

"Good candidate, my love," Mulisi said.

"Nay. He said he was from Shiloh." Mulisi's eyes lit up. "But he dropped not an 'h.'"

Mulisi threw back her head and laughed. "Imposter."

***

"We are not moving to Nineveh, Naqia," Yabu said.

"Mother, I have not asked you to accompany me to Assyria. All I am asking is that I be allowed to marry and move there with my husband."

"Pomie, Aki is to take my place as mayor; he cannot move to Assyria," Zakuta said.

"I do not wish to marry Aki. I wish to marry Damqi."

"Damqi!"

"Why would Damqi make you an offer of marriage," her mother said, raising a brow, "when he knows full well that you are intended for Aki?"

"He did not make me an offer. I made one to him." Naqia stepped back as her mother's face twisted in anguish.

"By the gods!" She threw up her hands and ran out of the room.

"Pomie," Zakuta said. "That will not do. I know you believe your destiny to be in Assyria. But it is your duty to remain in Damascus and marry Aki. This is the end of it. You have gone too far. Off to your evening chores while I see if I can comfort your mother."

Zakuta entered the sparse bed chamber that he had shared with Yabu for the past twenty summers. Yabu turned on him when he came in. "Who will wed her after news of this gets out? Offering herself to a man like that, what was she thinking?"

"You know our Pomie believes that she is to be in Assyria. I made it plain to her that she is to stay here and marry Aki."

"And if she refuses?"

"Refuses? I am her father."

"He who has made her the spoiled, useless female she is today," Yabu said, echoing her sister's concern.

"True, that. I will move up their wedding date. Will that console you?"

"Indeed. If she shows up."

Naqia stomped outside, she wrapped her arms around her body and paced. *How dare they refuse me? This is imperative. I must make Father see reason. Who cares if I do not marry Aki, as long as I marry someone?*

"Do you find him more appealing than you do me?"

"Oh, Aki. Go to your home. Do!"

"I shall not. Not until I find out why you intend to marry Damqi in my place."

"I doubt that you will understand."

"Why? Because I am content to succeed in the town of my birth? Because I do not have the drive and ambition that you possess? Which, by the way, is unnatural in a human female."

She turned to Aki. He had olive skin, a strong nose, though too prominent for her tastes, and a strong jaw. He wasn't a bad man, a little arrogant, but he had good morals. He would make a fine mayor. Still, he was not the man for her.

"Aki, I believe my destiny is in Assyria."

"As what? Damqi's wife?"

"I don't know exactly, but I must follow my heart."

Aki snorted. "As soon as you admit that you are a female—and not the son that your father has always wanted—the better off you will be, Naqia. For what role can you perform in Assyria that you cannot do here? Your duty is to marry, keep house and bear children. My children. It has been this way since Father Shem left the ark after the deluge."

"I intend to marry and bear children, Aki. But not yours, and not in Damascus." She left him standing there and went inside to finish her packing.

Men-nefer

Khaliut stopped his team of horses in front of the white-washed mud-brick walls surrounding the royal palace. Tirhakah waited for him at the entrance. Khaliut disembarked. "Tir, I have heard reports of your misbehavior. Are they true?"

"Yes, brother."

"How come you have taken to behaving in this manner?"

"I am so bored. The priest goes over the same lesson again and again. It is as if it is the only lesson he knows."

Khaliut rubbed his brother's shaven head as they headed inside. His uncle, King Shabaka, stood in the main hallway talking to his first aide. Khaliut drew near and bowed to his uncle.

"Pharaoh, if it pleases you, I have a report."

Shabaka gave his aide parting instructions before leading his nephews down the hall. Instead of the audience chamber, Shabaka led them outside to the garden. A small pool built in the garden's center had lotus blooms afloat. A turquoise peacock strutted around the garden.

"Nephew?" Shabaka took a seat on a bench.

Khaliut and Tirhakah remained standing.

"As you well know," Khaliut said, "each year after the harvest, Sargon consults his diviner about war. Shabataka asked that I travel to Nineveh to find out more."

Shabaka lowered his eyes. All became quiet for a minute. He looked up at Khaliut. "Dur-Sharrukin will be opening soon. They shall have days of celebration. You may attend and represent the Great House. Once the wine begins to flow, you may hear something useful. You are not, under any circumstances, to ask any questions."

Khaliut bowed. Shabaka waved him to a seat. Tirhakah moved to Khaliut's side, his eyes fastened to his royal uncle. *King. That is what I shall be someday. King of Cush. King of Kham.* "Royal Uncle, why must Sargon go to war after every harvest?'

"In Assyria, it is a ritual. The responsibility of the king to prove his manliness and ability to remain in power. Much like our heb-sed festival."

"It is rather silly, would you not say? To make war, solely for the purpose of appearances?" Tirhakah asked.

Shabaka smiled slowly, looking much like his late brother, Piye. "What will be your reasons for making war, Tirhakah, once you are king?"

"If my land and people were threatened, of course. What other reasons are there?"

"There are preventative wars," Khaliut said.

"Of course," Tirhakah said. "But I shall make war only if necessary. The kind of useless killing that the king of Assyria thinks necessary, I find offensive."

"It is not your place to be offended, Tirhakah, but the gods," Shabaka said.

***

The stench arising from the hay gave Naqia a headache. The donkeys harnessed to this rickety cart surely had slept on this hay at one time. Naqia gripped the sides of the wagon; now her forearms ached. In spite of her mode of transport, Naqia smiled. She had arrived. In Nineveh, home of the gods Sargon and Sennacherib. Here on the left bank of the Tigris River, the seat of the empire. This is where she belonged.

A surge of well-being flowed through her. The sense of destiny, which haunted her whenever the name "Assyria" was mentioned, made her heady. She could see high walls in the near distance, the walls of Dur-Sharrukin surely.

What a party they must have had. The wine must have flown freely. The food delicious, plenty of roast lamb. Every noble in the civilized world must have attended. I am furious to have been denied the pleasure. I am certain that my plans have suffered a setback due to my absence at Dur-Sharrukin.

"Here we are, madam." The driver called, halting the team. "Are you sure that your husband will be meeting you here?"

"You needn't worry, sir, I shall be fine until my husband arrives." She looked up at the inn. "You say that this is a respectable establishment?" *I will not suffer my reputation being marred by staying in a questionable inn.*

He brightened. "Yes, indeed. The crown prince, Sennacherib, comes here often for the cucumber soup." After more assurances, Naqia entered the inn.

"Good day to you, madam. I am Ashur-dan, proprietor of the Shiny Pomegranate Inn. It is where our future king dines."

I have not a whit of interest in the future king, but the present one. The Great One, who causes women to swoon when he but strides pass. "Thank you, sir. I require a room."

"Of course." He looked past her. "And your husband, madam?"

"He has suffered a delay. I assure you that I will be joined soon." Joined in matrimony, leaving your Shiny inn, and residing at Dur-Sharrukin. She flashed him a sweet smile. "My room, sir?" She handed him her basket.

He took the basket and led her down a narrow, torch-lit corridor. Naqia peered at the strange symbols inside the pomegranates marking the rooms. The spotless room smelled like a sage broom had just been used. An oil lamp sat on a three-legged stool. "Would madam like some heated water?"

"At once. Thank you, good sir."

Later, as she took a seat inside the dining area, Naqia understood why the inn experienced good traffic. She savored each drop of the onion and sesame soup; it had a hint of coriander in it, which reminded her of Yabu, who used to put coriander in almost every dish she made. Naqia felt a stab of regret, but she had done what fate required of her.

A Cushite couple sat next to Naqia. The woman munched upon rolled grape leaves with lamb. The man, who could be her father, ordered the same soup Naqia had. She could smell the coriander from his table—unless the cook was as liberal with the spice as her mother.

Odd that a Cushite couple would settle in Nineveh. The lands of Ham are as steady as a rock. Perhaps they are just traveling.

She turned her thoughts back to her plan. Her destiny. A royal union with the greatest war chief in the world: Sargon.

The thundering sound of racing horses startled the inn's diners. Some patrons stood up at their tables and peered out. Heavy armor clinking could be heard approaching the inn.

"It's Prince Sennacherib," a man at the window said. Two armored men with spears came in first.

"His Royal Highness, Prince Sennacherib," one said.

Despite her excitement, Naqia wrinkled her nose at the prince's entrance. *Was it necessary to cause a commotion at a mere inn? Did he think foreign dignitaries were present?* She appeared to be the sole foreigner, except for the Cushites, and they had retired to their room moments ago. She didn't notice their departure.

Naqia raised a slice of barley bread to her lips and watched as the prince sauntered in. *He is handsome, yes. But arrogant. A trait I find attractive in a man only if his deeds warrant it. Sargon, yes. His son? What has he done as yet? But what does one expect from the eldest son of the world's emperor?*

Sennacherib came to stand in the room's center, a slight tilt to his chin. The prince wore a tall, conical hat and a long robe with one arm exposed.

Ashur-dan wrapped a clean apron around his waist. He bowed before the prince. "Great Prince, how can I be of service?"

"What is your specialty of the day? Lamb with currants, I am hoping." Sennacherib's eyes swept lazily over the patrons. He spotted Naqia taking small bites of bread.

The innkeeper flushed. "I do have grape leaves with lamb, sir, but only a few left. And without currants, I am afraid. I didn't expect to see His Majesty this day." While Ashur-dan made his excuses, Sennacherib turned away and headed for Naqia's table.

"Greetings, beautiful."

Naqia laid her bread down and stood. She curtsied to Sennacherib. "Great Prince."

"Why is such a woman dining alone?"

"I am alone at present, my lord, but not for long."
Sennacherib's black eyes took her in from head to toe.
"From where do you hail?"

"Damascus, my lord."

"Was the soup to your delight?"

"Indeed, it was, my lord. Onion and sesame."

Sennacherib turned on his heels and headed for the door. "Innkeeper," he called across his shoulder. "I would wish grape leaves with lamb and currants on my next visit. As well as your wife's cucumber soup and barley cakes."

"As you wish, my lord," Ashur-dan said with a bow.

Sennacherib and his noisy guards departed the inn.

Naqia received admiring glances from a few female patrons. She sat down and congratulated herself for a successful encounter. *And on her first day in Nineveh, no less!*

The wagon, covered by animal skins, creaked up behind the Shiny Pomegranate. A white-haired man brought his team of donkeys to a halt. He jumped down and proceeded to unload baskets full of leeks, onions, and green herbs.

Ashur-dan stood in the doorway holding a lighted torch. Behind him waited a family of four from the auroch room. On signal, one at a time, they crept toward the wagon's rear and climbed inside. Joshua Ben Solomon and a young couple from the lion room followed.

Two brown-haired women, both plump, made long good-byes with Mulisi and Ashur-dan. Holding hands, the former cooks inched toward the wagon. The youngest, holding an olive branch given to her by her big sister, Mulisi, to signify their tribe if asked. When the three rooms emptied, nine people stuffed themselves inside the wagon.

The driver took his place in the seat. The wagon crept away; its occupants, Hebrew slaves, escaped Assyria to freedom.

Truly. This is an odd public house. Naqia waited a moment to make sure no one had seen her relieve herself. She didn't wish to be accused of spying. As it was, her "husband" had not shown up yet. She crept back upstairs to her room with the man on the pomegranate door and let herself in.

*****

I overslept! Tirhakah hopped out of bed and into a tepid bath. After a moment, he wrapped a kilt around his moist body and fastened it with a wide leather belt. He hurried pass the weaver's room, where the servant whistled at the loom. In his uncle's room, a body servant waited to apply kohl to his eyelids. Tirhakah hopped onto a chair, closed his eyes, and tilted his head upward.

"Where is the lad?" Shabaka asked his wife when she came outdoors carrying a pitcher of milk.

"He studied until dawn. Now he has overslept." She poured milk into a small cup and placed it at Tirhakah's seat.

"How many times have we told him about that? I shall have to resort to removing the oil lamp from his chambers."

The queen flashed him a sly smile, knowing that wouldn't work. "Will you be attending Tjanefer's class?"

"Yes, due to Tirhakah's misbehavior in class. Khaliut believes the lad is bored, so I shall visit this day."

"Morning, Aunt, Uncle," Tirhakah said, grabbing his milk and gulping it down.

Shabaka pushed his empty bowl toward the attending servant, who whisked it away. "Lad, how many times have I told you not to stay up past your bedtime? And before you give me your excuse, know that from henceforth I shall be removing your lamp from your room."

Tirhakah put the cup down and wiped the milk from his lip with the back of his hand. "But, Uncle, what if I have to get up and use the chamber pot?"

"The torchlight in the hall shall have to suffice."

"Good day, Aunt." Tirhakah ran back indoors, snatched his writing reed and palette, then ran all the way down to the river's bank and waited for his uncle.

The chamberlain came out into the garden and bowed before King Shabaka. "Your Majesty, we have a visitor from a foreign land."

"Now? Can he not present himself at the appropriate time?"

"Sir, he claims that his message cannot wait. It is most urgent."

Tirhakah watched reed boats sail pass. A few contained some of his schoolmates with their fathers, already en route to temple school. Few traveled to school via chariot in this season; the black soil remained slushy and bumpy with debris from the Nile's overflow.

Tirhakah tapped his foot. He loved to be the first pupil to arrive. *Oh, where is Uncle?*

Tirhakah sprinted the entire way back into the palace. He saw his uncle and the chamberlain enter the audience chamber. "A scribe is en route, Your Majesty."

"Oh, allow me, Royal Uncle. I am capable," Tirhakah said, hoping his behavior at school didn't undermine his uncle's belief in his learning.

"You may assist, Tirhakah." Shabaka turned to the chamberlain. "Who is this person? From what kingdom does he hail?"

"He is Isaiah, son of Amoz. He represents the Kingdom of the Most High."

Shabaka raised a brow. Minutes later, the chamberlain returned with a scribe and Isaiah. Isaiah, prophet of the Most High God, entered the audience chamber wearing sackcloth and plain leather sandals. Shabaka sat on his throne, a golden stool with leopard heads at both ends. The king's eyes traveled from the top of Isaiah's unkempt brunette head to his dusty feet.

The prophet wore no jewelry, no gold, not even an ornament to decorate his earlobes. Hair covered his shoulders, forearms, and legs.

Shabaka hid his distaste. "What kingdom do you represent? And why have you taken to walking around Kham with your buttocks exposed?"

"I hail from Jerusalem, Your Majesty,"

"Jerusalem? Has not Asshur put you asunder?"

"The Assyrians have removed our sister cities of Israel. Our tribes, Judah and Benjamin, remain. I am here to deliver a word to you, Shabaka, King of Cush and Mizraim, from the Lord of Hosts."

Shabaka gestured with his hand. "Go on then."

Shabaka's chariot sped toward the temple. Prince Tirhakah rode in a separate chariot with the king's first aide. Tirhakah didn't understand everything the prophet had said, but he knew the prophecy sounded grievous. Not just for Kham, but Cush as well.

The prophet will be preaching this message of doom for another two summers! How will they endure it? Royal Uncle intends to meet with his council after class.

They arrived as Tjanefer called out attendance. The priest's finger worked down his call list. "Menkare, son of Sebamon."

"Here, Priest."

"Tirhakah, son of King Piye, living forever!"

"Here, Priest." Tirhakah scurried to his spot.

The priest waited until the king's entourage settled down before beginning.

"Who are we, lads?"

"The sons of Ham."

"We descend from his son Canaan, do we not?"

"Indeed not, master. We are the descendants of Cush, first son of Ham. And Mizraim, second son of Ham."

"And who were Mizraim's children?"

"Ludim, Anamim, Lehabim, Naphtuhim, Pathrusim, and Casluhim."

"Very good. Pabasa, High Priest of Amon-Ra, will be our guest lecturer this day."

Pabasa gave a deep bow to the king. "Prince Tirhakah, young nobles. Get out your boards and pens. Today's lesson is most vital."

Shabaka planted one foot on top of his throne. He watched Pabasa, the Chief Vizier, and the Second Prophet of Amon discuss the prophecy. Shabaka interrupted them. "Nephew, read the first part again."

Tirhakah cleared his throat. "'Behold, the Lord of Hosts rides on a swift cloud and will come into Kham. The idols of Kham will totter at His presence and the heart of Kham will melt in its midst …'"

"Idols?" the vizier said. "Our gods represent our ancestors. Our priest-kings of old. It is who we are."

The Second Prophet spoke up. "And who is this 'Lord of Hosts?' To defame our ancestors. I do not know this God."

Shabaka said in a reverent tone. "Read the annals of Hatshepsut and Thutmosis III, living forever! And you shall meet Him." Shabaka paused. "The point is that He knows of us. And is displeased. Displeased enough to have one of His servants walking around with his backside exposed. Is there nothing we can do?"

"If the Lord of Hosts has purposed this upon Cush and Kham, there is nothing to do," Pabasa said.

Tirhakah took advantage of the silence to reread the portion that made his heart flutter. In a trembling voice, he said, "'the spirit of Kham shall fail in the midst thereof … they shall seek the idols, and the charmers, and them that have familiar spirits, and the wizards. And the Khamites will I give into the hand of a cruel lord …'"

"'A cruel lord'?" the vizier said. "Who can that be?"

Shabaka put his fists on his hips and turned from his council, making eye contact with his young nephew. "Assyria. Who else?"

***

Sargon strode down the palace corridor. Taliya waited outside the large double doors, wearing a floor-length gown and silver sandals. Her neck, ears, and arms were covered in jewelry. Inside, their guests waited for the great king and warrior chief to arrive and start the evening's festivities.

The palace herald announced his arrival. "Here cometh the great Sargon, beloved of Asshur, warrior chief of Assyria. Welcome Her Majesty, Queen Taliya."

Sargon strode into the hall with Taliya on his arm. An awed hush fell over the crowd. Prince Khaliut watched the king climb the short steps onto a blue and gold couch. Taliya sat opposite him on a high-footed chair. A fan-bearer took his position behind the king's headrest and fanned.

A stream of servants approached him offering honey-roasted pigeons, glazed dates, and the best wine in the empire.

Sargon raised a goblet of wine to his guests. The king's commanders-in-chief—Tartans—were assembled with their spouses. His generals, captains, and colonels stood with goblets of wine in hand, their bejeweled, decorated wives nearby. A few lesser army officers, who earned praise from the Great One, came upon his invite. Sargon's family stood in the crowd's middle, including his brother Sin-ah-usur.

The king lifted his chin. He was a monarch like no other. Fierce in battle, always victorious, and now he had a palace, a city unrivaled. He lowered his head in a rare act of humility and said. "For me, Sargon, who dwells in this palace, may Asshur decree as my destiny long life, health of body, joy of heart, brightness of soul."

"Hail, Sargon!"

The *Tartan* hurried down the corridor. He veered left into Sargon's audience chamber. The *Rabshakeh* stood there, wringing his hands. The *Tartan* did not slow his pace, but walked past the minister and said, "Walk with me." The *Rabshakeh* turned on his heels and followed into a courtyard.

They stopped near the fountain where water poured from the mouths of two huge stone lions. "This does not bode well, *Tartan*. Many saw him fall."

The *Tartan* turned to face him. "We cannot find the body."

The minister paled. His bottom lip quivered. "Sir, this will not do. What an omen! What a horrible sign!"

"Do lower your voice," the *Tartan* hissed, his eyes scanning the courtyard. "His Majesty took a direct hit in the chest."

"What are we to do? What if word of this spreads? Surely the Hittite who fired the shot is a hero. I would not be surprised if his monarch does not build him a villa in all twelve cities in Tabul."

"I am sure the Hittite king would have honored this warrior so. Had he lived. He fell soon after he slew our great king.

Despite our secrecy, word has spread. We must be off to Judah. The vassals are preparing to revolt against us. And Sennacherib says if his father's body is not found, he shall not take up residence in Dur-Sharrukin. This is a sign, surely that the palace, its city, and his father's reign have found disfavor in the eyes of the gods."

The minister bit his quivering lip; he said nothing, but his eyes agreed, growing round with fear.

Sennacherib lowered onto his father's throne with exaggerated grace. His wife, Naqia, straightened the purple gown around her extended belly and stood beside him. The nobles formed a line, depending upon rank and title, waiting for the new king, Sennacherib, to hear their pleas.

"We have little time, my lords, as the procession in my father's honor will soon begin," Sennacherib said. He kept his face stony, mournful. Indeed he must, for his new queen, Naqia, missed nothing. Already he feared that she suspected his elation about his father's demise. He gestured the first noble forward.

"My great king, Sennacherib. May Asshur grant you long life and good days. I come to you about a common complaint, one in fact your father heard in his time. The loss of revenue and indeed Apiru slaves. It has grown quite out of hand. I barely had the labor to bring in my last harvest! Something must be done."

"Let me put your fears to rest. I shall get to the bottom of the Apiru disappearing, and I assure you that, when I bring Judah to her knees, you will be provided with more Apiru slaves."

The noble bowed and moved away.

Naqia's mind drifted. Her husband's mention of the Apiru triggered a memory. Upon arriving in Nineveh, she had boarded at that strange inn. *Those odd symbols on the doors. Yes, of course. Apiru! They were symbols for Apiru clans. I shall return to the inn before the procession commences and take a look. If it is as I suspect, I shall bring my lord husband back to see for himself.*

Soldiers marched in precision down Nineveh's dirt streets. Flanked by his generals, Sennacherib lifted his chin and closed his eyes, allowing the exhilaration of power to fill his soul. He would command the world's fiercest army. He watched the funeral procession pass him. All the rebels had been punished save for one: Judah. Hezekiah will suffer, though, for his part in this conspiracy. The new monarch inclined his head and bid his father a silent farewell … wherever he may be.

***

Tenti waited until Ashur-dan crossed the small courtyard. The old man moved in front of him, blocking his entry into the inn. "Remember the Aramean? Pretty girl. Lived here quite some time until she realized her husband had deserted her. Now married to our Sennacherib?" Tenti said, glancing up at Ashur-dan through narrowed eyes.

"Yes. What of her?"

"She came by earlier this day with a troop of soldiers. Asking questions about your guests, and how some seem to disappear. She even went upstairs, snooping about the rooms."

"Guests disappearing? Is that what she said?"

Tenti did not care for the hardened look in the proprietor's eyes, but he grinned nonetheless and said nothing. He'd prefer his reward to come from the royal house, instead of an innkeeper. "I may be old and ugly, but I can still see." A pause ensued. Ashur-dan stiffened. Tenti waited, his chest rattling with each breath.

***

Jacob, also known as Israel and his twelve sons had swollen into a nation during their sojourn in Kham. Four hundred years later, twelve tribes emerged from Kham, subdued the land of Canaan, and birthed the nation of Israel.

Then came the tribal split, with ten tribes in the north retaining the name of Israel, while the remaining two tribes in the south—Judah and Benjamin—formed the nation of Judah.

Now, the ten tribes of Israel were separated from their brethren in Judah, having been conquered and enslaved by Assyria. Judah, though, yet remained free, with its capital in Jerusalem.

Jerusalem sat on a plain, nearly hidden by abrupt valleys. The Tartan, Rabsaris, and Rabshakeh traveled there from Lachish with troops. They stopped at an aqueduct along the highway, near the Fuller's Field. Their presence, with their gilded chariots, and gold and blue-jeweled robes, soon drew a crowd.

***

Justi poked around the cooking area sure he'd spot Mulisi standing on her tiptoes, stirring something in that kettle. *No one there. Strange. She is ill with the new baby, perhaps.* He moseyed over to the pot, leaned in, and sniffed. *Hmm. Barley stew. Nearly ready from the smell of it.*

He headed toward their home, peeled back the mat covering the door, and stuck his head inside. "Good morning, wee one. Your stew is done." He shuffled inside. *She must be here. She would never leave a good stew on the fire.* The home furnishings were bare. A bench. One small wood table.

Justi did not dare poke into their sleeping area. *They could be, uh, being man and wife.*

He went back outside, passed the cooking area to the animal pen. Gone. The goats, longhaired sheep, and lambs were all gone. Ashur-dan's covered wagon, nowhere in sight.

A blue-cloaked officer entered the Shiny Pomegranate. The inn tables were clean, with fresh palm fronds on each one, but only one customer was present.

An old man sat alone near the brazier, slurping stew. The officer took three long strides and stood over him. "Where are the owners?"

Justi swallowed. He looked up at the officer, blinking back the moisture in his eyes. "Gone."

More guards, accompanied by Naqia, came inside. "Search this inn thoroughly," she said. On the preparation counter, a few cooking utensils remained—but not Mulisi's favorite wooden spoon, Justi had noticed. The guards marched upstairs and opened the door to each room.

Naqia followed, anxious for another look at the strange emblems. The royal cultural minister had confirmed her suspicions. The symbols were known Apiru clan emblems. Now they were gone. Naqia ran a hand across the resin on the door. *My earlier visit must have warned them.*

Back downstairs, an officer sorted through Mulisi's grocery lists. He picked up one potshard and read in a whisper to himself: "'I, Susannah Ben Ephraim, the eternal optimist knew everything would be fine …'" He tossed it aside. He picked up another one, looking for a name, an ally, any clue to the owners' whereabouts. "'A prophet is coming. I told Ashur-dan this evening. Nineveh will fall this time. No mercy. All this warmonger—'"

The officer smashed the shard on the floor; then went outside to continue his hunt for clues.

King Hezekiah's staff—Eliakim, Shebna, and Joah—made their way through the crowd. The Assyrian dignitaries remained in their chariots. Cone-shaped hats sat atop long, black tresses. The Rabshakeh, a lieutenant to the Tartan, stepped forward and greeted the king's aides in flawless Hebrew. "My great king, Sennacherib, is no longer content with the amount of tribute your nation is paying."

Hezekiah's aides glanced at each other, startled, but said nothing in return. The Assyrian diplomat continued. "Tell King Hezekiah that our leader is puzzled by your sudden show of confidence. Is it true you now have better counsel and the strength to resist us—or was this merely an attempt to dissuade?"

The *Rabshakeh* raised his brows at their silence. "Very well then. We are certain that you have found an ally. Where is your nation placing its trust? I hope for your sakes that it is not Musri. True, they were once a great empire, but now they are a broken reed, which, if a man leans on, it will pierce him. That is what Pharaoh is to all who trust in him."

Eliakim tucked his head. Joah and Shebna continued to feign indifference.

The diplomat flashed a victorious smile at the *Tartan* standing next to him. "I can understand if your trust is in the Lord your God, even if Hezekiah did destroy His altars." The aides stared questionably at the Assyrian. The diplomat did not know that those altars were not Jehovah's, but erected for pagan worship by former kings.

The diplomat took a step forward and lowered his voice. "Listen, I must insist that you reason with my master. I will give you two thousand horses, that is if you can find enough men to ride them!" The Assyrians rocked back and forth with laughter. The Hebrews winced at the joke regarding Judah's small armed forces, but kept their peace.

The *Rabshakeh* held out his arms to them. "How can your nation resist even one captain in our army, and to trust in Musri for chariots and horsemen … it will not work. If you wish to know the truth, the Lord your God told us to come against your nation and destroy it."

The farmer had listened to the Assyrian boasts while sitting in his mule-harnessed wagon. He steered away from the Hebrew crowd. Once out of sight, he removed the cord around the heavy cloak and pulled the Hebrew garment over his head. The Khamite, a fair-skinned lad of Libyan descent, had proven his journey northward successful. He followed the Assyrians from Lachish to Judah's capital.

He drove down the Fuller's Field breathing easier the farther he traveled. His eyes watered from the smell coming from the fuller's trade. The lye, urine, and sodium solution the fuller used to bleach clothes caused his nose to run.

Now he had to rush back to Sin and report his findings to King Tirhakah.

***

Sennacherib left Lachish in shambles. He entered Libnah, twenty-five miles southwest of Jerusalem. His counselors arrived to find the king resting in his tent while the army leveled the Judean city.

"*Rabshakeh*, what do you know?' Sennacherib said.

"Your Majesty," he bowed. "Behold, Tirhakah, King of Cush and Musri, has come out to make war with you."

"Tirhakah, son of Piye?"

"Have no fear, great King. Musri does not have the might of old. Their arsenal is still of bronze and stone."

Sennacherib's brow creased. "Hezekiah thinks he is sly, does he not? When we have razed this town to the ground, we will head for his wee capital." He motioned for a messenger. "Send this message to Jerusalem. Ask Hezekiah what he is thinking. Look what the past kings of Assyria have done to other lands. Does he think to escape? Tell him to not let the God in whom he trusts deceive him."

He has not stirred himself to do a thing, the *Rabshakeh* mused to himself as Sennacherib prattled on to the messenger. *He is not the man his father was. The great Sargon led every battle, a war chief like no other. Now, though, were it not for our seasoned generals, we may have already encountered defeat.*

"*Rabshakeh*, quit your daydreaming," Sennacherib said. "I want a hundred thousand of our most hardened soldiers dispatched. When Tirhakah sees such a host, he will change his mind about making war with me."

The Khamite-Cushite army halted its march outside Judah. A messenger had been sent to inquire about Hezekiah's health and intent. Couriers sprinted back and forth, skirting through Assyrian defenses to report the battle's progress.

Tirhakah sat atop a large black stallion listening to the royal reporter's words. "The *Rabshakeh* told the Hebrews not to trust in Kham, a broken reed. He said a man will pierce himself by trusting in Pharaoh."

"And yet we are here, as our ally Hezekiah requested."

A Cushite messenger ran toward them. "King Tirhakah, live forever!" He bowed. "I have informed King Hezekiah of Judah that we have arrived to assist him against a common enemy, indeed an aggressive enemy toward the known world. King Hezekiah wishes you to know that he is fasting and beseeching his God for assistance.

Vizier Mentuehmat turned to his king. "I wonder that he sent for us, since he has such confidence in his God. Do you know Him?"

"He is the One whose hand smote Kham in the days of old," Tirhakah said, remembering his late brother Khaliut's information. The vizier flashed the king an awed look. "The Hebrews say He is the only real God. And there is no one like Him. Courier, send word to Hezekiah that we await his further instruction. We shall camp here."

After a day of warfare, the Assyrian soldiers slept where they fell. Some dozed off while trying to ingest the evening meal. The heat from the day lessened a bit into the evening, and many slept outside instead of in their tents. The camp became quiet and still right after sundown.

The angel slipped into the Assyrian camp. He glanced around at Sennacherib's pride and joy, his army. The angel departed, leaving 185,000 dead soldiers in his wake.

The *Rabsaris,* Chief of the Eunuchs and the *Rabshakeh* arrived to give the *Tartan* details for an assault on Jerusalem. In shock, they stood at the mass execution site, wondering if the scenario before them was genuine.

Sennacherib lashed out at his counselors. He refused to believe that his generals, captains, and soldiers were all gone. The king's face turned a deep pink underneath his olive complexion. "Are you certain they are all dead? Did you check? And the *Tartan*?"

"Your Highness," said the *Rabshakeh.* "They are all dead. What shall we gain from lying to our lord? Perhaps it was a plague of some kind, or some desert animals."

Sennacherib pounded his fists on his thighs. "That wiped out 185,000 men without a sound or struggle? Be sensible; it is not possible." We are disfavored by the gods. It must be so. First, father's body disappears. Now this. "We must return to Nineveh and beseech the gods of Assyria before we proceed further."

Tirone

Today

Bedouins rode camels along a mountainous ridge. Below them, bleached skeletal remains lay on the Nuweiban desert sand. Divers in wetsuits removed their gear. Photographers angled for the best shot. Researchers spoke in hurried tones into mini-recorders. Behind them, an American researcher stood holding a camera in midair.

The Bedouins sensed the foreigners' anxiety; they, too, knew that the Sinai Mountains would soon block the sunlight.

The bystander, clad in khaki shorts, dress shoes and socks, stood alone. His back faced the Wadi Watir range as he watched the workers lower a chariot wheel onto the sand. The axle remained intact but was now coated thick with coral. Seaweed cords wound themselves tightly around the eight-spoke wheel belonging to an eighteenth-dynasty charioteer.

Part of the Exodus fleet of six hundred. His worst fear realized, the bystander flipped opened his cell phone and punched the speed dial. The connection made, he raised the phone to his ear and spoke. "We have a problem."

***

Ah … The splendor. The glory. The magnificence of Kham. Tirone fingered the replica golden mask of Tutankhamon. He looked out at his classroom of thirty brown faces. Tirone Pulliam-Jones taught history at a Christian African-American prep school for boys. Sure, he focused on the usual topics in American history: George Washington chopped down the cherry tree. Paul Revere and "The British are coming!" And, of course, Harriet Tubman and Martin Luther King, Junior.

Fridays, however, were ancient history day. A time to pass onto these young brothers the knowledge about their ancestors before they were shackled together on those ships. The previous Friday, Tirone had brought a bow and arrow to class. He lectured on the Cushite bow troops: the Medjay. The students bombarded him with questions, taking frequent turns to touch the bow and arrow. One bespectacled lad drew a bow and arrow on his notebook cover.

For some reason, today's display on the boy-king Tut fell flat. *Overdone?*

Darrell King raised his hand.

"Yes, Darrell?"

"What happened to Nubia and Egypt? How come they aren't superpowers like America?"

"They used to be."

"Yes, I get that. But how come they aren't now?"

"There's no simple answer to that, Darrell. It would take an entire semester to answer that question. You would have to go into the wars they suffered, economics—"

"Did you check the Bible?"

Tirone stifled a sigh. *Why does everything with that kid come back to the Bible? True, the Old Testament has a lot to offer folks like me who study the ancient Near East. But as a Christian, if I can be bold and call myself so, the New Testament is it.* "I doubt this kind of information is in the Bible, Darrell. Maybe you should ask your parents." Tirone hoped the sarcasm in his voice didn't show. Mr. and Mrs. Darrell King, Senior, were self-proclaimed Bible experts. "My parents know all about the New Testament. It's your job as my teacher to teach me about history, like in the Old Testament."

"Well, you have asked a good question, Darrell. And I promise to look into it." The bell rang. Tirone watched his pupils use their feet and scoot back their chairs. Grabbing their books and binders, they scampered from the classroom. No school on Monday. Spring break!

***

"Mitch, I don't see this as a problem. There are plenty of slave-owning descendants around, many of whom have risen to prominence. Books can be written about these exporters of human flesh, both here and in Great Britain."

"Listen, I am running for political office. I don't need hordes of liberals asking me questions."

"Mitch, why would a relic from ancient history prompt modern questions? It's absurd."

"Not for a candidate with a record as clean as mine. Every blotch, no matter how old, can become a stain."

"You can always hold a press conference at the plantation. Look remorseful. Break out into tears. Show the world how sorry you are for our family's participation in the trade. And how, as a candidate, you will try to make the world a better place for all slave descendants—"

"I can't hold a press conference there. The house and other property holdings were paid for by legal and illegal means."

"But only we know that, Mitch. It isn't documented any-where is it?"

"No."

"Then let it rest. Historians cannot trace the slave trade back to us. The trail is too muddied."

***

Tirone let his laptop bag slide off his shoulder and onto the bed. *No papers to grade. Midterm exams have been returned, signed. All I have to do is relax, spend quality time with Paulie and plan the remaining semester's coursework.*

He hung up his coat, remembering to take the excess change out of its pockets. *Laundry money. Darrell's question was a good one. I may even write a book about it. Someday. But the answer won't be easy, and providing him one from the Bible ... near impossible.*

Tirone glanced at his nightstand, where he assumed most Christians kept their Bibles; but no, not Tirone Pulliam-Jones. He stored his Bible in a chest, inside the closet on a shelf.

He had purchased the chest at an antique shop in Cairo. He never tested it for a date. Of course, if Antiques Roadshow ever rolled into San Francisco, he'd have something to bring. He inched the chest forward and hoisted it down. The last time he had used the Bible, he dropped it back inside, and now it was lodged in sideways.

Good move, slick. Tirone shook his head at his silliness.

He gripped a corner on the Bible's binding and tried to lift it out. It budged a little, but the chest creaked. *Okay. This isn't worth breaking my chest over. I can always go out and buy a new Bible. This one's special, anyway, having seen four generations. Just a little more.* Slam. The chest's bottom crashed to the hardwood floor. Stiff yellow-brown papers cascaded downward.

Be cool, Ti, don't swear. He maneuvered the bottom back onto the chest. Grabbed the sheets and shoved them back inside. He sat it on the small garbage can, then picked up the Bible and went downstairs into the kitchen. He dropped the Book onto the kitchen table and headed to the freezer. He ripped a frozen pizza out of its cardboard box and placed it on the baking sheet he kept inside the oven, for the purpose of these gourmet meals, which he purchased in bulk.

A yellow notepad with his classroom notes, a couple of reference books, and a thirsty English ivy plant crowded the square wooden table. Tirone pushed the books aside and opened the Bible. *Where to begin?* He flipped back to page one, hoping for a detailed table of contents. No deal.

A few pages later portrayed a filled-in family tree. *And this is why I keep this little spiritual heirloom in such a special place. In case anyone ever asks why.*

The Bible belonged to his great-great-grandmother, Sadie McLean. Born in 1835, he read. *Outstanding.* Tirone reached for his notepad and a pen. He read through the notes, an arrow indicating to read the back. *She escaped from slavery? Did she go through the Underground Railroad? Why wasn't she in Canada?*

Tirone turned the page. An opening paragraph written in print followed sections in flowery handwriting. *Definitely a woman's hand.*

"I hope, reader, you are a descendant of mine. I want this Bible to stay in the family for reasons that will later become apparent. If you are not, but of African descent, please continue. This story is for you, too."

What is this? Tirone raised his head, letting the pen fall to the table. The oven hummed, indicating it reached the set temperature. Tirone stood to wind the oven timer, in case he became engrossed and burnt his meal. This happened more times than he cared to admit.

Tirone sat down and reached for the pen. *All right, Great-great-gran. Talk to me.*

"If you have read this far, you are curious. You wish to learn more. If you can stomach the truth—go back, curious

one. Connect the dots, if you will. Do not let the passing of time dismay you. That family, they are the craftsmen behind the African slave trade, make no mistake about it. It is for that reason I loathe to be mixed with them. And reader, if you are a descendant of them, please note: I loathe you as well.

Tirone made a left turn onto his street. His hand reached out and steadied a stack of library books on the passenger seat. He sped down into the subterranean parking lot in his apartment building, now condominiums. Tirone had moved here while still in graduate school, when the building had twelve apartments. After graduation he spent two years home in Mississippi while he waited for the renovations to be completed.

In the bedroom, he threw his jacket on the valet chair. The sheet from the old chest still lay on the garbage can. He felt torn in three directions: Take a closer look at this; it may be ancient. Answer Darrell's question. Or find out what Sadie meant … "I loathe you as well."

He jogged downstairs into the kitchen and made a pot of coffee; then went into his office. *Okay. I don't have time to procrastinate.* He uncapped his favorite black pen. I have to find the answer to Darrell's question. He searched through the Bible, this time armed with a Bible concordance—and a quick prayer for divine assistance. He found a clue in the book of Isaiah. "The idols in Egypt will totter …"

Idolatry. That's interesting. No self-respecting historian would ever list that as a reason for an empire's demise. But Darrell wants a spiritual reason for Kham and Cush's fall, and here it is. But this may be too deep for ancient history Fridays. I'm going to need to break this down for the little brothers.

Tirone quit reading and stared out of the window. Last summer, the neighbors' ten-year-old boys had roped a tire to the tree, separating their home from the condominium complex. Now they swung back and forth on the tire, bare-chested and in shorts, welcoming spring.

His thoughts returned to Sadie. He opened the desk drawer and pulled out a lined notebook pad. He wrote a sentence then another. In five minutes, he'd written two pages. He stopped. He hated writing about those bullwhip days. He ripped the pages from the pad and set them aside. *Back to ancient times. Back to the fall of Kham and Cush. This has to be done before spring break is over.*

Tirone's doorbell rang. He opened the door for Paulette. "What's up, Prof?" She came in orange, high-wedged sandals, her twisted hair secured by an African-themed hair band.

"Nothing much. A little research, a little writing."

"Professor, it is Saturday night. Take me to dinner."

"All right, pushy sistah. Let me tidy up." They entered his office.

"What are you working on?"

"If I tell you, we'll never get to the restaurant. But here, read this excerpt in my Bible."

Paulette faked a surprised expression. "You own a Bible? When did ya go out and buy one of those." He dropped the Bible into her outstretched hands. She buckled. "Geez."

"Let's not go there. Read my great-great-granny's notes while I take a quick shower."

Paulette raised her brows, letting her eyes scan his desk. "What else can I read? Hey, I can never get you to read a sistah's poetry."

"Paulie-luv, you know I hate poetry something fierce. Read these five pages. They're based on biblical prophecies against Kham and Cush."

"No way." She dropped into his seat. "I didn't know that was in the Bible."

"I'm ashamed to admit it, but neither did I. Be back." He jogged out of the room.

Paulette read Sadie's notes first. "'I loathe you as well,'" she said out loud. She glanced to her left to see if Tirone had gone upstairs. He always made fun of her speaking aloud to herself.

Paulette turned the page. "Oh, sistah, tell me more. I'm curious." The note ended. "Aw!" She heaved the Bible onto the desk and picked up the two pages Tirone had written earlier.

"I'm selling this." Paulette turned the pages facedown. She picked up her utensils and sliced a meatball.

Tirone sipped a glass of white. "I thought you'd gone vegetarian?"

"Hmm. Not this week. When can you finish this?"

"I dunno. I'm sure I can get a chapter or two written during spring break."

"Two chapters? That's it? Brother, I have clients who can write a full chapter in an hour."

"Well, I'm not a professional author, am I? Besides, this is all based on prophecy, and I'm no biblical scholar."

"You have a PhD in Near Eastern and African studies. Get out of here. Anyway, it'll be nice to have a male client. All five of my authors are females." She pointed her fork at his veal. "Are you going to eat that?"

***

McLean slid into the all-white breakfast nook. Glad to be home, he smiled as he faced the same breakfast he ate every morning: a flax-and-bran muffin, grapefruit, and black coffee. He opened The New York Times to the best-seller lists, mainly out of habit.

He knew his latest book had climbed into the top five. His eyes scanned down the nonfiction list for *We, Modern Israel.*

The book had raised another notch, now listed at number three. Were it not for those chariot findings, he would feel elated, if not a bit smug. Especially toward the agents and publishers who told him there was no market for his work. He had proven them wrong.

He knew his target audience. They were not vocal about their beliefs, not wishing to be affiliated with hate-groups who also believed. But rest assured, his audience spoke in volumes, keeping his books in demand.

Fortunately, he hadn't taken the "fame" route. He refused all but one talk show, limited his promotion to like-minded radio programs and private party lectures. Still, his name was known. He was the man, the kook as one book reviewer said, who believe he descended from the lost ten tribes.

So far he had avoided making a statement to the press about the chariot. But now he had an upcoming book signing. He checked his watch. He needed to get to the neighborhood bookstore and see if *We, Modern Israel* were well stocked.

Main Street embraced the bright spring morning. Small white, pink, and lavender flowers burst from window boxes gracing shop windows. Yellow daffodil and pink tulips were on display in front of the grocery store.

McLean parked his black Lincoln Town Car. Outside the bookstore, a man in a suit smiled as he approached. McLean searched his mind, trying to place a name with the grinning face.

As he grew closer, McLean realized the man was not smiling, but smirking. A reporter, from some liberal rag, no doubt.

"Good morning, sir. I am Adam Pendicott, reporter for the Times. Gotta question for you."

McLean rattled off the name and cell number of his publicist.

"I read your books, sir. I know who you are. Or rather, who your people once were. The African slave trade became an organized business under your ancestors' direction. Was it revenge, sir?" The reporter aimed a small tape recorder at McLean.

"I have no response, Mr. Pendicott. Thank you." McLean hurried into the bookstore, his face flushed red. Two brown winged chairs sat adjacent to the cashier's counter. McLean eased down in one, resting his liver-spotted hands on his knees.

The bookstore owner, Mr. Erman, approached. "Dr. McLean, can I get you a glass of water?"

"Thank you, William. That would be nice."

Why should I be dismayed? I knew this would happen. Brother thinks I'm daft to think that history, ancient or otherwise, can come back to haunt the modern.

McLean felt himself being watched. He looked up to see a slender African-American man standing in the history section. The man lowered his head into the book he held before sneaking a glance at McLean. Like he debated what he should do. McLean eased his reading glasses out of his shirt pocket.

Is that one of my books he has? Not that I mind, though he wouldn't be considered my audience. Does he want an autograph?

In the bookstore's history section, Tirone snapped the book shut. The book outlined the economics behind the African slave trade. No mention made of "that family." But that older gentleman over there … Mr. Erman called him "Dr. McLean"—the same surname as Sadie.

It couldn't be. I mean, I've heard of divine appointments, but this is too much. Don't quite know if I can bring myself to talk to this man. I've never read any of his books, solely on principle, but I know who he is.

He is a McLean, born and raised in Mississippi. Tirone sighed. *Well, I may not remember much in the Bible. But Gramps always said that God hates cowards.*

McLean watched Tirone approached. He straightened, this time prepared to defend his ancestors if necessary. *After all, why should he shoulder the blame? He wasn't there.*

"Morning, Dr. McLean. I heard Mr. Erman use your surname. I wonder if you have time for a question."

"What newspaper do you work for?"

"None, sir. I am a history teacher. My great-great-grandmother Sadie McLean left a family Bible …"

McLean's red face receded. He paled at the implication. He had assured his brother there was nothing written down. At least not on public record. "And?"

"Sadie McLean escaped slavery, but her family may have worked your ancestor's property in Mississippi. She left a very depressing letter behind for her descendants so I was wondering if you had any information on her. I'm anxious to learn anything else."

A letter? That's it? Still, the question remains, what else did she say in that letter? McLean put his face in his hand. *Why me? Why now? Why couldn't my ancestors, say after the Emancipation, deal with the mess they made? Why leave it up to posterity?* "I tell you what, young man, what is your name?"

"Tirone Pulliam-Jones."

"I tell you what, Mr. Jones. Here's my business card. When you're ready, I'll give you a copy of Sadie's memoirs."

"Seriously?" Tirone took the card.

"Yes. Seriously." McLean thought it time to face his ancestors' choices head on. Truth be told, he and his family still lived quite well, getting a good start from the slave trade. *My ancestors, the bondage brothers. "The Bondage Brothers." My goodness, that's it. My next book. It shouldn't take long to write, and if my agent pushes, I can have it out before campaigning begins. Come forward and confess this slavery business once and for all.*

Sunday evening found Dr. Mitch McLean in his office hard at work. His wife, Clara, had attended a fund-raising event without him. He couldn't possibly go.

"Why not?" she had asked.

"I have to write this, and I need to do it fast."

Mitch had skirted around the real issue: he feared Sadie's letter. Mr. Jones would write her story. He needed his book to come out first. But should it be nonfiction, or should he try his hand at fiction? Perhaps both then see what works the best in the end.

I should've asked Mr. Jones whether or not he'd secured a literary agent. It's unlikely he has one, and who knows ... perhaps the teacher cannot write well enough. He may not get an agent. At least that would give me the time to get my book out before his.

Mitch rubbed his upper lip. *Where to start?* He stared at the burgundy leather-covered penholder, holding a dozen sharp pencils. He would use each one to write in longhand before moving to his computer.

Clara McLean entered her husband's office. Bookshelves on both ends were full; one shelf above the computer held his books, bound in leather. Two life-sized portraits of his ancestors hung on the walls. A woman with russet hair piled high, wearing a low-bodice gray gown could have been Clara's ancestor, both having the same color of hair.

The second portrait portrayed a man in a powdered wig; he wore a white frilly shirt underneath a blue overcoat.

Mitch sat rolling a dull pencil between clasped hands. She lifted her skirt and sat on the edge of the desk. "No mention of your chariot findings at the fund-raiser."

"What about the club? Didn't you go after church?"

"I could've been in Bermuda for all you know. No, no one mentioned it at the club. And if Ed and Cynthia don't know, then the furor has died down."

"Neither Ed nor Cynthia are reporters for The NY Times any longer. I'm sure plenty of things escape their attention nowadays."

"I doubt that. They remain close with their former peers. What are you writing anyway that hasn't been covered in your previous books? Surely, you didn't uncover any new research with the chariot?"

He handed her a stack of pages. She read for a moment then wrinkled her nose. "This is fiction."

"Yes, I know."

"But why?"

He dropped the pencil. "It wasn't a conscious effort, I assure you." He shrugged. "It came spilling out of me like that." He swiveled away from the desk and rose. "I need to stretch my legs. Do you want some coffee?"

She swung her legs off the desk. "Please." She sat down in one of the leather chairs facing the desk and continued reading.

***

Jazz music played in low volume. Paulette stood at the kitchen's island slicing zucchini. Tirone's green "Let's BBQ" apron, a housewarming present from his parents, was tied around her waist.

Tirone sat at the table typing on his laptop. Beside him sat the Bible and an assortment of historical texts. Two manuscripts, which Paulette had to find time to read this evening, sat at the opposite end. The manuscripts blocked the English ivy's continual cry for attention.

Paulette opened the oven and slid out the chicken to baste. Tirone paused. "The Scriptures don't tell whether or not the prophet Isaiah told the pharaoh about these prophecies."

"You're writing fiction Prof. You can take the prophet anywhere you need him to be."

Tirone chuckled. "I don't want to rewrite history."

"You're not. You're embellishing it." She put the chicken back in the stove and lowered the oven's temperature. "You can always write it as nonfiction."

"True. Are you ready for me to set the table?"

"In a few." She took the seat in front of the manuscripts. "I need to get started on these."

"Isn't this an exciting evening?"

"Hmm. Quite romantic."

Tirone laughed. He clicked the "save" icon, then stood and stretched. He opened the utility drawer and found two white taper candles. Paulette looked up from her reading when she heard him rummaging through the drawer trying to find the candleholders.

She smiled and lowered her head. Finally, he lit the candles and sat them on top of the Bible concordance. Paulette smiled up at him. "Magical."

After dinner, Paulette juggled a tray with two mugs of Irish crème coffee, a platter of wafer cookies, along with a five-hundred-page manuscript, and headed to the office. Tirone followed with his laptop and books. "I bet you that by the time school resumes, Darrell would've pestered his parents about his question."

Paulette dropped the manuscript on the two-seater couch. "Or he's forgotten all about it. Do those little brothers actually pay attention to your ancient history lectures?"

"If I embellish them. Bring in props. Throw in a little warfare complete with horses and chariots. Otherwise they'd get bored. One Friday, I lectured on the religious changes brought about by the pharaoh Akhenaton."

"Tirone! Come on. You're lucky they didn't make paper balls and throw them at you."

"Paper balls can't fly."

"Well, airplanes then. Geez."

The phone rang. Tirone eased his load onto his desk and picked up his landline. "Hello. Hey, Mama, how you be? No, no worries. Paulie and I are having dessert." He listened on the other end for a moment, then laughed. "No, Mama, I haven't proposed yet."

Paulette burst out laughing. Tirone shot her a sheepish grin. After more pleasantries and Tirone asking about his sister Ona's new baby, he remembered Sadie. "Mama, do you recall hearing about an ancestor who escaped from slavery "by passing" for white?"

"Yes—Sadie," she said. "Tirone, do you ever read that Bible of yours? It's full of family history."

"I know, Mama. I just stumbled on it again. I've been trying to find out what she meant by loathing her descendants."

"Humph. Well, I think she wrote that before everything worked out between her and Mr. Livingstone."

"Ah, I see. Anyway, I met a McLean today, a real-live slave-owning descendant."

"What!" Paulette shouted from the couch.

"Is that right?" said his mother. "Did you say anything to him?"

"Yep. I asked him about Sadie—"

"And what did he say?"

"He said he had her memoirs, and I can have a copy whenever I like." In the background, Paulette snorted in disbelief.

"Memoirs? Boy, your ancestors didn't have time to be writing no memoirs. That man is gonna write his own version of events. Sadie is gonna be a happy, singing slave. Glad of the backbreaking work and in love with the massa when he's done."

"I didn't think of that. But he can't do too much harm, since Sadie was free."

"I just remembered, your cousin Sheila started writing Sadie's story as fiction. Make sure you compare this McLean's version with hers, 'cause she's living with her great aunt Patty, and they have firsthand accounts of what happened."

"Thanks, Mama, I will do that. Give everyone my love. Right. Talk soon. Bye-bye."

Tirone hung up and told Paulette what his mother said about Dr. McLean.

"Mama knows best," Paulette said.

"Well, I need to put Sadie aside anyway and focus on Darrell's question."

***

McLean walked his golden retriever along the wide tree-lined street. In this neighborhood, few cars traveled the road. The fog had dissipated; a few streaks of morning sunshine came peeping through the trees. McLean's running shoes crunched dead twigs on the pavement. Golda, the retriever, kept the sixty-year-old moving at a steady clip.

It would be quite remarkable if the fiction continues to flow. I've never written fiction in my life. I wonder if my agent would approve of this departure. "Your track record," he's sure to say, "Is in nonfiction. Your readers would expect more along the lines you've always written."

Well, this isn't actually a departure. I'll complete three chapters and email them to him. That way he can say whether or not to continue, shelve it, or redo it as nonfiction.

McLean gazed up at the clear blue sky. In the distance, mountains could be seen. If someone traveled in the other direction for a few miles, he or she would encounter the beach. McLean's country club and favorite seafood restaurant were in that direction.

From the restaurant's second floor, one could view the dolphins leaping up and diving back into the ocean. McLean smiled. Something clicked in his mind. He reached into his tracksuit pocket and took out his mini-recorder. He pressed "record" and continued the story.

***

Tirone took the bowl of Corn Flakes into his office. The phone rang. He looked at the number on the screen. "Morning, Paulette."

"Good morning, Professor. Are you finished?"

"Finished? I just started breakfast. It is spring break remember? I ain't about to roll out of bed at five a.m. for another few days."

"I ain't talking about your breakfast, ninny. Have you finished the book?"

"Naw, I haven't finished the book. I'm still researching Darrell's question."

"And you're going to try to write that as fiction?"

"For now. It helps me to understand the time and order of events. Who knows where it'll lead?"

"On the bottom of my slush pile, that's where."

Tirone swallowed then laughed. "Look, Ms. Agent Extraordinaire, I could have two books in me."

"Hmm. Well, I have things to do before noon. I have a new client to lunch and munch with."

"When do I get to be wined and wooed?"

"When you finish writing that book! Now back to work, Prof."

Slave driver. Tirone finished his cereal, taking the pleasure of slurping the milk since he lived alone. Mama wasn't here to turn from the stove and flash him "that look."

He didn't want to tell Paulette, but he had actually finished another chapter, inspired from reading the book of Isaiah. He turned on the computer. While he waited for it to boot, he picked up the phone receiver and punched in his Great Aunt Patty's digits.

"Hullo, Great Auntie, how you be?" Tirone listened and laughed at his aunt's comments before he asked. "Is Cousin Sheila around? I wanted to know if she finished writing that book about our ancestor Sadie McLean."

"Naw, she ain't finished," Aunt Patty said. Tirone could hear his uncle in the background correcting his wife of forty years about her grammar. "Why do you wanna know about that now? Its ancient history."

"I'm trying to find out why she was so mad. She was free, right?"

"Barely. Her mother was freed by the owner. But Sadie had to serve a few years. And she never got a copy of the papers, though. From what I heard told, the family had a copy but wouldn't give it up."

"You mean the McLean family still has those papers?"

"Yeah. And they prove that Emma McLean, Sadie's ma, was free, and so was Sadie."

"So those years she served were illegal."

"Exactly." Tirone said his good-byes and hung up. *No wonder she was hating. I am not mad at you, Great-great-gran. Not at all.*

Tirone rubbed his scratchy eyes. He rose from the kitchen table and went into the living room. He sprawled out on the couch. *I'll just take a quick nap. I'm on ancient overload here. I have lived and breathed in the eighth century BC for too long.*

And school starts back tomorrow. No worries. I have more than enough for Darrell King. Ruining my spring break with his question …

Tirone sat in his office at the school. His computer screen displayed the next examination, a mixture of contemporary events and ancient history questions learned from the past Friday's exhibit.

A knock sounded on the door. "Come in," he said. *Must be Darrell's parents. He probably told them that he had a teacher who knew nothing about history and the Old Testament.*

He turned his attention away from the computer and stood to greet the visitor.

A young woman, dressed in a simple cardboard brown frock, sat in the chair opposite him. He hadn't heard her come in. Her shoulder-length hair appeared shiny and perfect, too perfect. It must be a wig, or a weave. Her big brown eyes stared through him, like she was studying him and looking past him at the same time. *Eerie.* Heavy kohl lined her eyelids, along with heavy blue eye shadow.

"Good morning," Tirone said.

She smiled, confused.

"Are you Mrs. King? Darrell's mother?"

She paused then said, "I am Nenksen-amon."

Tirone blinked. *Another African-American mother who let creativity get out of hand.* "What can I do for you, Ms. Nenksen-amon?" Another long pause ensued. She seemed to be digesting his words. *Perhaps English isn't her first language; she does have a heavy accent.*

"You have something. The papyrus—I should like you to read it to me. Tell me what it says about my beloved."

Tirone narrowed his eyes. *Did she say papyrus?* "Why?" he said, slower. "What is in the papyrus you wish to see?"

"I need to find out what happened to my beloved."

Tirone decided to play along. "Where did you last see your beloved?"

"He boarded his chariot and left Men-nefer in your service." *Chariot? Men-nefer? Ancient Memphis?* "My service?"

"Are you not Tirhakah, living forever?"

"I am not. I am Tirone, his descendant."

The buzzer on the oven sounded. Tirone jolted awake. He smelled pepperoni, sausage, and melted mozzarella. *Now that was just weird.*

Tirone washed his lunch plate, rinsing out the soda can and tossing it into the recycling bin. *Paulette was right. I should've written it as nonfiction. No worries, I have good notes and did most of the research, so now I can go back ... The chest!*

Tirone threw the dish towel on the table and jogged upstairs into the bedroom. He grabbed the sheets from the chest and flopped down onto the bed.

Some were written in Aramaic, the other in hieroglyphs. *Hot diggity.* He spotted the cartouche at the top of one sheet. *Tirhakah. King of Cush and Kham.* He lowered the sheets and stared into space. *No way.* He raised the sheets to his eyes and translated the first lines under the king's throne names. *This is unbelievable.*

"We fell. Despite the warnings given of our demise, no one believed. Not even I. We should have heeded the prophet's dire utterances, disposed of the idols in both Cush and Kham."

Tirone ran back downstairs into his office, grabbed a brand-new yellow lined notepad and a pen. His blood felt like it was pumping at warp speed. He wanted to yell and do somersaults all at the same time.

With care, he placed the parchments atop an in-file drawer; then took out one of the sheets written in Aramaic. He reached for his reference books and dictionaries in ancient Hebrew, Aramaic, and Egyptian.

"You are reading this. If you are reading this, then it has happened. My narratives were copied. How exciting. First let me introduce myself. I am Mulisi, wife of Ashur-dan. We run an inn here in Nineveh ..."

Tirone paused and re-read his Aramaic-to-English translations. He grimaced. *It will do. I can take it to my old department head at the university later.*

"How exciting it is that you are reading this. I have jotted down my narratives for several summers, and I have given them to a priest here in Men-nefer in hopes that he will have them copied and distributed. These narratives are going to be a success. Of that I am sure. Like 'The Shipwrecked Sailor,' or 'The Story of Sinhue.'

"They shall be read by priests to students all over the Assyrian world, and Kham, well, everywhere I am sure. Before you read on, let me assure you that these narratives are truth. As an innkeeper, I served many important people. I was a part of history, you shall see."

Whew! Tirone exhaled. *This ancient woman knew how to write? Then she was no ordinary innkeeper. I hope all of her narratives don't have this kind of energy.*

He searched through the parchments for others in Aramaic, thus written by this innkeeper named Mulisi who lived in Men-nefer. *They didn't do signatures in those days. None would say "Mulisi" at the bottom.* He rechecked the one he had just read. At the bottom was depicted a symbol. *Is it a bull? An ox? It looks familiar. Huh ... wait, there's one more narrative.*

***

Susannah Ben Ephraim, eighteen summers old stepped outside her home. "Good goat!" She said aloud. *All is well.* She gazed around the village of her birth, Janoah; its stony desert populated with fig trees and pomegranate shrubs. Four women walked pass the petite wine seller standing barefooted and all smiles in her doorway.

See there. I knew everything would be fine. The prophet who uttered Israel's demise? Drunk, probably. Surely a false prophet. I mean, good goat. How many times can Israel be taken captive? Were we meant by God to be an enslaved people? Certainly not.

Susannah grabbed her water jug and skipped toward the well. *G-d made a covenant with us. We are His covenant people. Not that we were chosen for our good looks; or our vast numbers.* She snickered at her humor. *No, G-d said we were the least of all peoples in the earth. The smallest nation there is.*

Susannah hugged the earthenware jar against her chest. More women approached en route to the well. Their conversations punctuated with nervous laughter. Janoah did appear well, but the village trembled. Susannah felt the vibrations under her bare feet.

Warfare for three years straight made her accustomed to the sounds. The air reeked of burned homes, though Susannah never seen a real fire. Muted screams, moans and anguished cries had blended in with the village's everyday sounds.

She approached a round stone altar. Incense spirals rose from its mouth. A fragrant offering dedicated to heathen gods, not the G-d of Israel, petitioning them to save Israel. Indeed, if the prophet of G-d is to be believed, Israel will not win this war.

It would be unfair, though, for all of Israel to suffer punishment. I do not worship idols nor does my Nathaniel. Why should we be punished?

A sheep waddled passed her. A barking dog echoed in the distant. The sight and sound afforded a sense of normalcy. Soon it would be time to harvest the olive crop. Susannah's eyes darted from side to side, searching for another good sign.

The trembling she felt in body and mind was due to the prophet's dire prediction, to Nathaniel being in the thick of the fighting, and to the recent death of Caleb, her youngest brother. Nothing more.

Two stick-thin boys raced past heading toward the well. A family led two packed mules toward the village's gate. *They are leaving Janoah. Surely, they are only going to visit kin nearby. Maybe friends in Manasseh. Or are they heading to Judah, for the safety of Jerusalem? How are they to get past Asshur? Surely the Assyrians have blocked the exits.*

All the same ... Susannah filled her jug and hurried home, where Nathaniel had instructed her to stay in the first place. *Surely, he did not expect me to stay indoors all day, every day. I could wither and die if I do not get out and about. Talk to people. Maybe sell a wineskin or two.*

Susannah felt her usual joviality return. She considered going back to the well to see who else was there, what they were feeling. "How is life? How are you and your family coping with the war?" she imagined herself asking.

All will be well. I, Susannah Ben Ephraim, eternal optimist, mind you, am certain.

The shofar sounded. Susannah heard the crashing of water jugs. She didn't turn around to look. Her tiny feet smacked the ground as she sprinted home. She dropped the water jug on the ground in front of their one-room home and ran inside. Nathaniel turned and scowled at her. She blushed. He was chopping off his brown-blond locks.

Why is he doing that? That was not part of the plan. Or was it? Susannah's heart dropped. She knew at once all was lost. The prophet proved correct.

Susannah scurried about like a confused chicken. She stuffed family mementos and her favorite wooden cooking spoon inside her drenched smock. Nathaniel shoved out of his farmer's tunic and wrapped a kaunake around his waist, its sheepskin fleece faced outward. They'd rehearsed this scenario countless times, but as usual Susannah improvised.

Nathaniel hated that.

He used one arm to gather her to him. Then he ripped away the items she so carefully tried to conceal. Susannah looked up at her husband. His set jaw gave her pause. She realized this was a side to him she'd never seen. The side he reserves for his military errands. The last was a fact-finding trip to Assyria on behalf of Israel's now-dead king, Pekiah.

Nathaniel forced a new dress over her head, much heavier than the dull beige smock she wore daily. He had sewn in silver coins. He led her outside without a word. Assyrian soldiers stood on guard at the village gates. They would be exiled. The prophet had indeed uttered the word from the Lord. Israel would be leaving the Promised Land.

Nathaniel dragged her behind an oak tree, keeping a tight grip on her forearm. Susannah wondered what they waited for. She watched her kin people, Ephraimites, red-faced and sobbing as they were herded into a single file to march away from a defeated Israel.

Susannah let out a yelp. Nathaniel clamped his hand over her mouth. Her parents and sisters trudged by. *Where was her father? And elder brother? Not dead, surely. G-d, have mercy.*

We are not idolaters. She sobbed. *G-d. Truly, we did not offer incense to Baal. We did not carry shabti dolls. We are not the guilty ones, G-d. Her chest heaved with sorrow. We served You alone.*

Dusk came and Assyrians were still marching from house to house dragging stragglers out, and forcing them into the exodus. Weak from sorrow, Susannah lay slumped against Nathaniel's thigh. She had seen his immediate family depart, and cousins as well. It was all too much. *Surely, his grandmother would not survive the trek to Assyria. I shall never* see any of them again. She wrapped both arms around Nathaniel's thigh and held on tight.

As they remained hidden, a long break in the procession occurred. Susannah thought it all over. They would return to their home and leave for Judah when all was safe. Instead, Nathaniel dragged her into the next wave of departing captives. He posing as a soldier in Tiglath-Pilesar's army, and she a Hebrew captive.

***

Tirone let the papyrus fall to the desk. He clasped his hands as in prayer. *McLean believes he's descended from these people. No way. These are not their ancestors.* He remembered his dream. *I am Tirone, Tirhakah's descendant. The king of Cush and Kham lived in the eighth century BC, as did this Mulisi. Why was she living in Men-nefer? If she was Jewish, she should have been an Assyrian slave.*

Tirone fished out the chapters he'd written, flipping back the yellow pages until he found a blank sheet. Then he wrote…

***

The royal chronicler parted his blue robe and squatted down. He unrolled a blank scroll, dipped a reed pen into the ink palette and waited for his lord to speak. Esarhaddon, king of Assyria, sat upon his throne, stretching his short legs out before him.

The walk from his chambers to the audience room left his breathing labored. He would not allow it to be witnessed though, not on this day. His mother, Naqia, would notice. Today he would set the record for all to see, his victory in Musri and triumph over Cush.

Esarhaddon closed his eyes, waiting for his breathing to return to normal. He let a small smile play on his lips. His advisors, generals, and royal brethren would know he had no concern for his health. Instead, he relished the remembrances of Tirhakah's defeat.

He took a deep breath and opened his eyes. "Tirhakah, king of Musri and Cush, is vanquished. I fought bloody battles against him, accursed by Asshur, Shamash, and indeed all the gods of Assyria."

Esarhaddon paused. "Five times I hit him with the point of my arrows, inflicting wounds from which he should not recover. I plundered his palace, and removed his wives, sons, and daughters. As well as the seed of the house of his father, the son of the earlier kings."

The nobles cheered. However redundant the news, the Cushite royal family had indeed been presented at Court two sunrises ago and given spacious homes to live in.

The king continued. "Indeed, the root of Cush is uprooted from Kham. Tirhakah's lineage is finished, for he is surely dead."

***

Tirhakah's bandaged body lay upon a goose-feather bed. A wrinkled woman, a Khamite, sat in the room's corner mending his bloodied, torn cloak. *Why does the woman trouble herself? When I return to battle, I would wish a new one.* The Cushite king's skullcap and cane rested on a chest underneath a window.

Esarhaddon of Assyria proved victorious. If he is like his father, Sennacherib, then he gloats, mayhap he prances about in the manner of a peacock. Braggart. Tirhakah smiled. *But I know something Esarhaddon does not. His gods, Shamash and Asshur, may favor his brutal, bloodthirsty ways. There is One God who does not.*

The memory gave Tirhakah a thrill. Inwardly, he felt peace, like his body repaired itself, infused with the mere know ledge. *Esarhaddon is too young to remember, but I saw the One God's displeasure. Yes, 185,000 Assyrians slaughtered as they slept. Boastful, proud, and prepared to smash King Hezekiah's Judah upon daybreak. Assyria received a sample of what she so greatly deserves. Assyria is neither invincible nor is she highly favored. She will fall, and soon.*

"Esarhaddon, King of Assyria, take heed," Tirhakah said aloud. The woman in the corner raised her head and listened. "We will never die."

"Tirhakah, King of Cush and Kham, live forever!" the Khamite responded. The king relaxed; he needed his rest. Before he flew to Osiris, Tirhakah vowed he'd give Esarhaddon one last thing to think about.

The Egyptian woman examined the cloak. Two blood splotches had faded to a dull brown, but the rest she managed to remove. She draped the cloak across her knees; the sparrow-hawk of Cush remained unscathed.

She clucked her tongue. *Aye, that is a good sign.* She had let the cloak dry in the house, directly under a spot in the front room where the sun beamed in full. No one must know the king recuperates here. Men are men. A Khamite would take Assyrian silver in exchange for information like anyone else.

She entered the chamber where the king lay asleep with a pleasant look on his face. *He dreams of happier times. He does not know that his palace had been plundered. Or that his family has been carted away to Assyria. When he is stronger, he must be told. Right now, he must rest.*

The woman folded the stiff cloak, and laid it inside a plain wooden chest; which she once used to store her late husband's kilts. She cleaned it out especially for the king's personals. Five arrow wounds, he suffered. He will not using *these anytime soon.* She placed his skullcap and gilded walking stick inside.

Tirhakah opened his eyes and smelled burning charcoal, baking bread, and cooking fish. He remembered that the pleasant memory of Assyria's destruction had lulled him to sleep. The God of the Hebrews exacting vengeance against Asshur; next time He would destroy their entire army.

This God, He intervened for King Hezekiah, but not for Pekiah, king of Israel. Are they not brethren? The royal reporter said God became displeased. Did the mighty God of Israel say the same for Cush, and indeed the land of Ham? He did.

Is this defeat our punishment for worshipping false gods, and indeed our ancestors? Who said this?

Tirhakah searched his mind. The picture returned. An unadorned foreigner, a Hebrew, stood before Uncle King Shabaka and delivered a word from the Hebrew God. *Isaiah, I believe his name was. I was a lad when this dire predicament against Kham and Cush was uttered. Isaiah. Yes, that was he.*

An entire summer passed, the inundation rise gave the Khamites renewed hope, despite the foreigners now administering in the Black Land. When the waters receded, farmers drove their ox- and mule-led carts through the moist soil, sowing lettuce and barley seeds.

The Khamite woman tending the fallen king sat on a stool and watched Tirhakah sip the last drops of emmer and goose porridge. She had added onions to the mixture, but he ate heartily and did not seem to mind.

The king's physical wounds healed well. The five arrow holes closed with no sign of infection. The monarch's heart, however, did not fare well. He longed for revenge. From Ra's rise to descent, Tirhakah thought of nothing else.

Alas, if I do not succeed, he thought. *I wish my people to understand why. It is the Great God's decree. He who wields more power than Amon-Ra, but chooses to use the small nation of Hebrews as His vessel.*

"Papyrus and pen," he said, handing the empty bowl back to her.

"Shall I fetch you a scribe, Majesty?" The entire village now knew the old woman had a lodger; no one could eat as much food as she cooked daily.

When pressed, she admitted to nursing a wounded soldier back to health. "A soldier befallen by the cruel, merciless Assyrians," she would add for emphasis. A few neighbors had asked to meet this warrior, a hero in the Black Land. No, she would insist. Visitors may delay his progress.

Tirhakah sat up straighter, leaning his bald head against the wall. "No, madam I am able." The words sparked a memory. When he was a lad of seven or eight summers old, he stood in for a real scribe on behalf of his royal uncle, Shabaka.

Fresh tears came to his eyes; he remembered his family taken hostage to Assyria. His Chief Queen Diketamani, and Queens Yusata and Qualhata. His son, Nesishutefhut, Second Prophet of Amon resided in Kham. The last he had heard, Ushanakhurru his son with Queen Yusata was at his studies in Men-nefer. He shut his eyes to stem the tears. The sorrow did not soften his heart. Though it strengthened his resolve.

To my people. To the clans and tribes that reside under the Royal Hawk of Cush. To the clans and tribes that reside in the Black Land, the land of Ham, under the Royal Falcon. Take heed. The Great God commands us to put aside idola try. We will fall. We shall never rise again. But we shall never die.

Tirhakah placed the papyrus aside. "We will never die."

"Live forever," said the Khamite.

***

The moment he sat down, Darrell King raised his hand.

"Yes, Darrell."

"Did you find the answer to my question? You had two weeks."

"So did you. What research have you done?"

"I'm too young to do research."

"Says who? You can read, can't you?"

"Of course."

"Then you can do research. So here's your assignment. Everyone get out your notebooks and jot down the following Scriptures. We are going to spend the next few weeks helping Darrell research his question."

\

Historical Notes

King Nefertkumkhure Tirhaka was born in Feburary 722 BC. I tampered with his age for the story's sake. At the time of his father King Piye's death in 712 BC, Tirhakah would have been aged ten.

Cush, also known in recent times as Nubia, is located in the Sudan. Bible translators refer to Ham's eldest son as Ethiopia.

Mizraim, second son of Ham, is modern Egypt. In Scriptures, Mizraim's name is synonymous with "the land of Ham." (See Psalm 78:51, Psalm 105:23, Psalm 105:27 and Psalm 106:22)

Canaan is today's Palestine (Israel). The curse on Canaan (a servant to Shem) was fulfilled when Joshua led the Israelites into the Promise Land.

This author believes that Ham's last born son Phut resided in the land Punt; and the land called Libya was founded by Mizraim's son, Lehabim. Alas, many scholars identify Phut as the founder of Libya, so I have left it as so.

Marcella Denise Spencer

www.ingramcontent.com/pod-product-compliance
Lightning Source LLC
Chambersburg PA
CBHW060640130626
46555CB00002B/887